English Grammar Juncture

英文文法階梯

康雅蘭
嚴雅貞／編著

- 升高一必備的英文文法教材，奠定深厚基礎功力
- 說明扼要搭配簡潔例句，文法觀念一點就通
- 每回附有豐富練習題型，幫助學習高效吸收

三民書局

國家圖書館出版品預行編目資料

英文文法階梯／康雅蘭, 嚴雅貞編著.－－修訂二版
十六刷.－－臺北市: 三民，2024
　　面；　公分.－－（文法咕嚕Grammar Guru系列）

4710660289740　（平裝）
1. 英文語言─文法

805.16　　　　　　　　　　　　　95002090

英文文法階梯

編 著 者	康雅蘭　嚴雅貞
創 辦 人	劉振強
發 行 人	劉仲傑
出 版 者	三民書局股份有限公司 (成立於 1953 年)

三民網路書店
https://www.sanmin.com.tw

地　　址	臺北市復興北路 386 號　（復北門市）　(02)2500-6600
	臺北市重慶南路一段 61 號 (重南門市)　(02)2361-7511
出版日期	初版一刷 2003 年 10 月
	修訂二版一刷 2006 年 3 月
	修訂二版十六刷 2024 年 2 月
書籍編號	S804630
	4710660289740

序

如果說，單字是英文的血肉，文法就是英文的骨架。想要打好英文基礎，兩者實應相輔相成，缺一不可。

只是，單字可以死背，文法卻不然。

學習文法，如果沒有良師諄諄善誘，沒有好書細細剖析，只落得個見樹不見林，徒然勞心費力，實在可惜。

Guru 原義指的是精通於某領域的「達人」，因此，這一套「文法 Guru」系列叢書，本著 Guru「導師」的精神，要告訴您：親愛的，我把英文文法變簡單了！

「文法 Guru」系列，適用對象廣泛，從初習英文的超級新鮮人、被文法糾纏得寢食難安的中學生，到鎮日把玩英文的專業行家，都能在這一套系列叢書中找到最適合自己的夥伴。

深願「文法 Guru」系列，能成為您最好的學習夥伴，伴您一同輕鬆悠遊英文學習的美妙世界！

有了「文法 Guru」，文法輕鬆上路！

給讀者的話

　　「英文文法階梯」是專為剛升上普高技高的新鮮人所編寫的英語學習書籍，希望幫助高一同學對英語基本的文法概念有清楚且整體的認知，並為未來三年的高中英語學習打下良好的基礎。

　　為了達成這個目的，我們在編寫的過程中盡量摒除過於艱澀，或高二以上才有機會首度接觸到的文法概念。全書以句型輔以簡明解說，不只教師能以本書作為高一的文法加強教材，採用本書的自修者也能在最短時間內有效吸收基礎文法概念。

　　本書各章節均自國中已學過的文法觀念開始延伸，以收溫故知新之效。每一小節後的 Try This 與章末的 Test & Review 則提供讀者演練文法的機會，請讀者務必親自作答，切實檢討，方收加深印象之效。

　　至盼經由本書的幫助，能協助高一同學站穩英語學習的腳步，更有自信的迎接未來三年的挑戰。

Table of Contents

Are You Ready?

1–1 五大基本句型

在學習英文時，有「完整句子」的概念是很重要的。一個完整的句子結構裡，應該包括主詞 (S) 和動詞 (V)，而依據動詞的性質不同，可歸類出五大基本句型。以下將針對這五大句型做詳細的解說。

一、主詞 + 完全不及物動詞

句型： **S + Vi**

說明： 這類型的句子最主要是在強調主詞所做的動作，例如：come, go, leave, arrive, rain, snow, sleep, sit, lie, work, laugh 等，可用表示時間、地點的介系詞片語或表狀態的副詞來修飾。

Examples:

1. They laugh.　　　　　　　　　　　　　　（他們笑了。）
   S　　Vi
2. Joyce came to school today.　　　　　　（Joyce 今天來學校了。）
   S　　Vi
3. He left without telling the teacher.　　　（他沒有告訴老師就離開。）
   S　Vi
4. It rained suddenly on my way home.　　（在我回家的路上突然下雨。）
   S　　Vi
5. I worked hard all day.　　　　　　　　（我整天都努力地工作。）
   S　　Vi

注意 不及物動詞是不接受詞的，如例句 1。但接了介系詞之後，即可接受詞，如例句 2。

二、主詞 + 不完全不及物動詞 + 主詞補語

句型： **S + Vi + SC** (N/Adj)

說明： 這個句型的動詞以 be 動詞與連綴動詞為主，必須要接主詞補語 (SC) 來補充說明主詞的特性或狀態，此類常見的動詞包括：be, become, seem, remain, keep, stay, look, feel, taste, smell, sound, fall, turn, get, grow, appear 等。其中 be 動詞、stay 或 remain 的後面可以接地方副詞作補語，用以表示「所處位置」。

Examples:

1. $\underset{\text{S}}{\text{I}}\ \underset{\text{Vi}}{\text{am}}\ \underset{\text{SC (N)}}{\text{a nurse}}$.　　　　　　（我是一位護士。）

2. $\underset{\text{S}}{\text{Tom}}\ \underset{\text{Vi}}{\text{became}}\ \underset{\text{SC (N)}}{\text{the class leader}}$.　　（Tom 成為班長。）

3. $\underset{\text{S}}{\text{He}}\ \underset{\text{Vi}}{\text{seems}}\ \underset{\text{SC (Adj)}}{\text{angry}}\ \text{with me}$.　　（他好像對我很生氣。）

4. $\underset{\text{S}}{\text{She}}\ \underset{\text{Vi}}{\text{will be}}\ \underset{\text{SC (地方 Adv)}}{\text{here}}\ \text{right away}$.　（她馬上就會到這裡了。）

5. $\underset{\text{S}}{\text{She}}\ \underset{\text{Vi}}{\text{remained}}\ \underset{\text{SC (地方 Adv)}}{\text{in her room}}\ \text{all day}$.　（她整天都待在自己房間裡。）

Try This!

I. 以下皆為 S + Vi 或 S + Vi + SC 的句型，選擇適當的動詞使句意完整。

☐ 1. They (A. kept B. arrived C. fell) at the airport late. The plane had left.

☐ 2. I was (A. angry B. turned C. angrily) with myself for doing such a stupid thing.

☐ 3. Honesty is the best policy. You shouldn't (A. lie B. talk C. tell) to me.

☐ 4. Everyone (A. feels B. grows C. comes) nervous on stage.

☐ 5. We (A. moved B. waited C. made) for him patiently.

II. 以下皆為 S + Vi + SC 的句型，從框中挑選適當的答案放入句中，使句意完整。

(A) kept	(B) tastes	(C) remain	(D) getting	(E) felt

1. It _____ raining all day yesterday. Kids had to stay at home.

2. Why not call Mary tonight? She is supposed to _____ at home all night.

3. The children _____ surprised when their teacher took them to play outside.

4. The weather is _____ hot and humid.

5. The cake _____ sour. You'd better not eat it.

三、主詞 + 完全及物動詞 + 受詞

句型：**S + Vt + O**

說明：許多動詞如 like, love, enjoy, believe 等作及物動詞時，必須要接代名詞、名詞、名詞片語或名詞子句當它的受詞。

Examples:

1. <u>Her plan</u> <u>shows</u> <u>her intelligence.</u>　　　　　（她的計畫顯示出她的智慧。）
　　　S　　　 Vt　　　　O (N)

2. <u>I</u> <u>don't know</u> <u>where to go.</u>　　　　　　　　（我不知道要往哪裡去。）
　　S　　 Vt　　　O (N 片語)

3. <u>She</u> <u>didn't believe</u> <u>that Oscar was a girl.</u>　　（她不相信 Oscar 是個女孩。）
　　S　　　 Vt　　　　O (N 子句)

四、主詞 + 不完全及物動詞 + 受詞 + 受詞補語

句型：**S + Vt + O + OC**

說明：不完全及物動詞除了接受詞以外，還需要接受詞補語，才能使語意完整。不完全及物動詞可分為兩類，<u>一種是可接名詞、形容詞或分詞作為受詞補語的</u>，像是 have, make, get, keep, find, think, consider, believe, leave, drive 等；<u>另一種則是只能接名詞當受詞補語的</u>，像是 call, name, elect, choose, appoint, declare 等。

Examples:

1. Jack <u>had</u> <u>his hair</u> <u>cut</u> yesterday.　　　（Jack 昨天剪了頭髮。）
　　　 Vt　　 O　　 OC (分詞)

2. His bad grades <u>made</u> <u>his mother</u> <u>angry</u>.　（他的壞成績讓他媽媽很生氣。）
　　　　　　　　 Vt　　　 O　　　 OC (Adj)

3. Nancy <u>kept</u> <u>me</u> <u>waiting</u> for one hour.　　（Nancy 讓我等了一個小時。）
　　　　 Vt　 O　 OC (分詞)

4. They all <u>call</u> <u>Miss Wang</u> <u>a walking dictionary.</u>　（他們都稱王小姐為活字典。）
　　　　　 Vt　　　 O　　　　 OC (N)

五、主詞 + 及物動詞 + 間接受詞（人）+ 直接受詞（事、物）

句型：**S + Vt + IO + DO**

說明：這個句型中的動詞通常稱為「授與動詞」，例如：give, bring, send, buy, show, ask, build, do, find, get, order, tell, prepare, fetch, lend 等，需要接兩個受詞（通常一個是人，一個是事物）句意才能完整。

Ⓔxamples:

1. My boyfriend bought me a bunch of roses. （我男友買給我一束玫瑰花。）
   <u>Vt</u> <u>IO（人）</u> <u>DO（物）</u>

2. She didn't tell him the truth. （她沒有對他說實話。）
   <u>Vt</u> <u>IO（人）</u> <u>DO（事）</u>

3. He asked me a question. （他問了我一個問題。）
   <u>Vt</u> <u>IO（人）</u> <u>DO（事）</u>

在這句型當中，直接受詞和間接受詞的位置是可以互換的，先接直接受詞（事物）的話，在間接受詞（人）的前面必須加上適當的介系詞，像是 to, for, of 等。

Ⓔxamples:

1. My boyfriend bought a bunch of roses for me. （我男友買給我一束玫瑰花。）
   <u>Vt</u> <u>DO</u> <u>Prep</u> <u>IO</u>

2. She didn't tell the truth to him. （她沒有對他說實話。）
   <u>Vt</u> <u>DO</u> <u>Prep</u> <u>IO</u>

3. He asked a question of me. （他問了我一個問題。）
   <u>Vt</u> <u>DO</u> <u>Prep</u> <u>IO</u>

I. 選擇適當的答案使句意完整。

☐ 1. I love (A. it B. X C. very much).

☐ 2. The computer doesn't work properly. We must have it (A. repairing B. repaired C. repair).

II. 依照提示回答下列問題。

1. A: What does your brother fetch for Mark? (*sports magazines*)
   B: He _____ for him.

2. A: What did Mary lend to you? (*some money*)
   B: She _____ me _____.

1-2 主詞與動詞的一致

一、單一主詞與動詞的一致

單一主詞與動詞的搭配最主要取決於主詞的單複數，請看下列的類型和例句。

類型 I

> All/Most/Some/Half/A lot/
> Plenty/Part/The rest
> 分數／百分比
> + of +
> 單數名詞／代名詞 + 單數動詞
> 複數名詞／代名詞 + 複數動詞

注意 主詞的單複數一般是決定動詞的主要因素，另也有特例喔！

Examples:

1. Most of my money is spent on comic books. （我大部分的錢都花在漫畫上。）

2. Some of the countries were against the war on Iraq. （有些國家反對對伊拉克開戰。）

3. One-fourth of the students like swimming. （四分之一的學生喜歡游泳。）

4. Sixty percent of my time was occupied by homework. （我百分之六十的時間都被功課給佔滿了。）

類型 II

> 單數名詞 + 介系詞片語 + 單數動詞
> 複數名詞 + 介系詞片語 + 複數動詞

Examples:

1. A list of books and their writers is given to the student. （這學生拿到一張列有書名和其作者的單子。）
   ⇨真正的主詞是「一張單子」。

2. Two famous writers from the United States are visiting Taiwan next week. （兩位來自美國的知名作家下週將訪問台灣。）
   ⇨真正的主詞是「兩位知名作家」。

類型 III

> class/family/audience/government/
> committee（委員；委員會）/team/
> staff（工作人員）/jury（陪審員；陪審團）

+ 單數動詞（表示整體）
+ 複數動詞（表示團體中的成員）

（**注意**）動詞的單複數可看出主詞強調的是整體或其中成員。

Examples:

1. The audience <u>is</u> not satisfied with the show.　（觀眾對這場表演並不滿意。）

2. The audience <u>are</u> all girls.　（觀眾都是女孩。）

3. My family <u>has</u> lived here for 10 years.　（我們家已經在此住了十年。）

4. My family <u>are</u> all well.　（我的家人都很好。）

類型 IV

> something/nothing/everything/
> anything/someone/nobody

+ 單數動詞

Examples:

1. Anything <u>is</u> possible for her to do.　（任何事她都有可能做得出來。）

2. Someone <u>is</u> singing outside.　（有人在外面唱歌。）

將括弧內的動詞改為適當的形式，使句意完整，請以現在簡單式做答。

1. The news about their winning ＿＿＿＿＿ (*make*) us happy.

2. Two-thirds of the land ＿＿＿＿＿ (*belong*) to the government.

3. Part of his story ＿＿＿＿＿ (*seem*) unreasonable.

4. The staff in this restaurant ＿＿＿＿＿ (*serve*) the customers well.

> 類型 V

| the + 形容詞 | + 複數動詞 → 指的是「某一類的人」。

Examples:

1. The poor are not always unhappy.　　　　　（貧窮的人並不總是不快樂。）
2. The old need to be taken care of.　　　　　（老人家是需要被照顧的。）

> 類型 VI

| there is + 單數可數名詞／不可數名詞 |
| there are + 複數可數名詞 |

Examples:

1. There is a program about designing robots on TV. （電視上有一個關於設計機器人的節目。）
2. There are several policemen in the park.　　（公園裡有幾位警察。）

> 類型 VII

| many a + 單數名詞 + 單數動詞 |
| many + 複數名詞 + 複數動詞 |

（**注意**）many 後面有沒有 a 是影響動詞的關鍵。

Examples:

1. Many a young lady wants to stay fit.　　　（很多女人都想保持身材。）
2. Many men like to play golf.　　　　　　　（很多男人都喜歡打高爾夫球。）

> 類型 VIII

| the number of + 複數名詞 + 單數動詞 ⇨「…的數字」 |
| a number of + 複數名詞 + 複數動詞 ⇨「一些…」 |

注意　the number of 指的是「…的數字」，所以要接單數動詞。

Examples:

1. The number of traffic accidents increases sharply.　（交通事故的數字急速增加。）

2. A number of workers decide to go on a strike.　（有一些工人決定要罷工。）

類型 IX

時間／距離／重量／價值　+ 單數動詞

Examples:

1. Four years is too long a period to wait.　（四年等起來太久了。）

2. Twenty miles is a long way to run.　（要跑二十哩是很長的一段路。）

3. One million dollars is a large amount of money.　（一百萬是一大筆錢。）

Try This!

I. 根據主詞選出正確的動詞形式。

☐ 1. The homeless (A. need B. needs) a place to stay overnight.

☐ 2. The number of tourists (A. increase B. increases) sharply.

☐ 3. Many a man (A. hope B. hopes) to make his dream come true.

☐ 4. One hundred dollars (A. are B. is) too much for such a dress.

☐ 5. There (A. are B. is) no money in the purse.

II. 將括弧內的動詞改為適當的形式，使句意完整，請以現在簡單式作答。

1. A number of students ＿＿＿＿＿＿ (be) studying English in the classroom.

2. Many a young man ＿＿＿＿＿＿ (make) the same mistake.

3. The number of students who ＿＿＿＿＿＿ (want) to buy this dictionary ＿＿＿＿＿ (be) increasing.

4. Six hours of sleep ＿＿＿＿＿＿ (be) not enough for a child.

5. The sick ＿＿＿＿＿＿ (be) looked after by experienced nurses in this hospital.

二、兩個主詞與動詞的一致

兩個名詞藉由連接詞合併作主詞時，連接詞的使用會影響到主詞與動詞之間的一致性，大致上有以下的類型：

類型 I

單數名詞 and 單數名詞 +
- 單數動詞→表同一人、物、觀念
- 複數動詞→表不同人、物、觀念

Examples:

1. Bread and butter is my favorite food. （奶油麵包是我最喜歡的食物。）

2. Bread and butter are not on the shopping list. （麵包和奶油都不在購物單上。）

3. Two and four are/is six. （二加四等於六。）
   ⇨數學加法用 and 時，接單複數動詞皆可。

類型 II

no/each/every/many a + 單數名詞
and (no/each/every/many a) 單數名詞
+ 單數動詞

Examples:

1. Each man and each woman is afraid of getting sick. （每一個男人女人都怕生病。）

2. Many a man and many a woman enjoys exercising. （許多男男女女都喜歡運動。）

類型 III

either A or B　　　　　（不是 A 就是 B）
neither A nor B　　　　（不是 A 也不是 B）+ 動詞【與主詞 B 一致】
not only A but also B　（不只 A 還有 B）

Examples:

1. Either you or I am wrong. （不是你就是我是錯的。）

2. Neither you nor Mary needs to come tomorrow. （你跟 Mary 明天都不用來。）

3. Not only my uncle but also my parents are in Japan. （不只我叔叔還有我爸媽都在日本。）

類型 IV

A +

as well as	（和）
with	（和）
together with	（和）
along with	（和…一起）
but	（而不是，除了）

+ B + 動詞【與主詞 A 一致】

Examples:

1. You <u>as well as</u> he <u>are</u> chosen as best workers.　　（你和他都被選為最佳員工。）

2. <u>Everyone</u> <u>but</u> <u>you</u> <u>has</u> to attend the meeting.　　（除了你，每個人都得參加會議。）

三、非名詞的主詞與動詞的一致

以不定詞（to + 原形動詞）、動名詞 (V-ing)、名詞子句（that 子句）或名詞片語（疑問詞 + 不定詞）等為句子的主詞時，所接的動詞皆為單數動詞。

Examples:

1. <u>To drink a lot of water</u> <u>is</u> important for our health.　　（喝很多水對我們的健康是很重要的。）

2. <u>Walking a dog after dinner</u> <u>makes</u> John relaxed.　　（晚餐後溜狗讓 John 放鬆。）

3. <u>That the sun rises in the east</u> <u>is</u> a fact.　　（太陽從東邊升起是個事實。）

4. <u>How to solve the problem</u> <u>troubles</u> us.　　（如何解決這問題困擾著我們。）

Try This!

將括弧內的動詞改為適當的形式，使句意完整，請以現在簡單式作答。

1. Neither they nor Jessie ＿＿＿＿＿＿ (*borrow*) Mr. Lin's cell phone.

2. Where to spend their holiday ＿＿＿＿＿＿ (*trouble*) George and Mary.

3. The boss as well as the employees ＿＿＿＿＿＿ (*refuse*) to work overtime.

✓ Test & Review

I. 選出正確的答案。

☐ 1. Either Mary or I _____ to take the responsibility.

(A) have   (B) has   (C) am   (D) is

☐ 2. That the earth is round _____ a fact.

(A) have   (B) has   (C) is   (D) are

☐ 3. A number of doctors _____ diagnosing patients for free.

(A) are   (B) is   (C) has   (D) have

☐ 4. Each boy and each girl _____ to take notes in class.

(A) need   (B) are   (C) have   (D) has

☐ 5. There _____ more than two answers to this question.

(A) is   (B) are   (C) has   (D) have

☐ 6. Two-thirds of the juice _____ drunk by Lisa.

(A) have   (B) were   (C) has   (D) was

☐ 7. The mayor made sure that the sick _____ properly taken care of.

(A) was   (B) is   (C) were   (D) have

☐ 8. The news of his passing the entrance exam made the whole family _____.

(A) excitedly   (B) excited   (C) satisfying   (D) laughing

☐ 9. The cake my mother made tasted _____.

(A) sourly   (B) deliciousness   (C) well   (D) sweet

☐ 10. They consider Jerry _____.

(A) smart and hard-working   (B) wisely and honestly

(C) lazy man   (D) diligently

II. 根據下列句子選出正確的句型。

☐ 11. My grandparents lived in the country before they died.

(A) S + Vt + O   (B) S + Vi+ SC

(C) S + Vi   (D) S + Vt + O + OC

12. I found my money stolen when I came home.
    (A) S + Vi   (B) S + Vi + SC
    (C) S + Vt + O   (D) S + Vt + O + OC

13. Driving too fast is very dangerous.
    (A) S + Vi   (B) S + Vi + SC
    (C) S + Vt + O   (D) S + Vt + IO + DO

14. The pirate told his fellows where to find more treasure.
    (A) S + Vi + SC   (B) S + Vt + O
    (C) S + Vt + O + OC   (D) S + Vt + IO + DO

15. We considered Michael a nice teacher.
    (A) S + Vi   (B) S + Vi + SC
    (C) S + Vt + O   (D) S + Vt + O + OC

III. 根據中文完成英文句子。

16. 老師和學生都不知道什麼時候才會有水可以用。

The teacher _____ well _____ the students _____ know _____ they will have water to use.

17. 很多女孩子都喜歡寫信或寄自己做的卡片給她們的偶像。

Many a _____ _____ writing letters or _____ handmade cards _____ their idols.

18. 告訴孩子什麼是對的和什麼是錯的是父母的責任。

Telling children what is right _____ what is wrong _____ the responsibility of parents.

19. 半數的委員們很不高興地接受這樣的結果。

_____ of the committee _____ not happy to accept the result.

20. 愛人也能被愛是每個人都想要的。

To love and to be loved _____ what everyone _____.

2-1　時態的意義及形式

在英文裡，動詞的使用會因為時間的不同而有不同的變化，這種因為時間的不同所形成的動詞變化，就稱為動詞的「時態」。一般而言，我們可以將時間簡單地區分為「現在」、「過去」和「未來」三種；而動詞的形式則分別有「簡單式」、「進行式」、「完成式」和「完成進行式」四種。

時間 \\ 形式	現　在	過　去	未　來
簡單式	I learn English.	I learned English.	I will learn English.
進行式	I am learning English.	I was learning English.	I will be learning English.
完成式	I have learned English.	I had learned English.	I will have learned English.
完成進行式	I have been learning English.	I had been learning English.	I will have been learning English.

2-2　現在式

一、現在簡單式： 在英文裡，現在簡單式可以用來表示「現在的事實、狀態、習慣或動作」以及「不變的事實、真理或格言」等。

「現在簡單式」的動詞形式	be 動詞	"am"（主詞為第一人稱單數）；"are"（主詞為第二人稱、複數名詞）；"is"（主詞為第三人稱單數、單數名詞）。
	一般動詞	原形動詞（主詞為第一、二人稱、複數名詞；主詞為第三人稱單數、單數名詞時，動詞字尾加 "s" 或 "es"。）
	助動詞	和一般動詞連用於「否定句」或「疑問句」，助動詞後的動詞一律用原形。其中，"do" 用於主詞為第一、二人稱、複數名詞；"does" 用於第三人稱單數、單數名詞。

1. 第三人稱單數的現在簡單式，除了 be 動詞用 is，have 改為 has 外，其他的動詞字尾都加上 s 或 es。
2. 表示習慣性的動作時，句中常會出現頻率副詞如：always, usually, often, sometimes, never 等。

<< 表示現在的事實、狀態、習慣或動作 >>

Examples:

1. I am in Taiwan. 　　　　　　　　　　　　　（我在臺灣。）
2. Is it hot now? 　　　　　　　　　　　　　　（現在很熱嗎？）
3. They often take a walk after dinner. 　　　（他們常在晚餐後散步。）

<< 表示不變的事實、真理或格言 >>

Examples:

1. The earth goes around the sun. 　　　　　（地球繞著太陽運轉。）
2. To see is to believe. 　　　　　　　　　　　（眼見為信。）

<< 助動詞 do 用在否定句或疑問句 >>

Examples:

1. I don't like to watch soap operas. 　　　　（我不喜歡看肥皂劇。）
2. Do you know that boy? 　　　　　　　　　（你認識那個男生嗎？）
3. Does Sophia get used to the life in the U.S.? 　（Sophia 習慣美國的生活嗎？）

Try This!

根據中文完成英文句子，請以現在簡單式作答。

1. Andy 每天都看英文報。Andy ＿＿＿＿＿＿ English newspapers every day.
2. Stanley 不喜歡讀書。Stanley ＿＿＿＿＿＿ ＿＿＿＿＿＿ to study.
3. 你們每天都做運動嗎？＿＿＿＿＿＿ you ＿＿＿＿＿＿ exercise every day?
4. 天助自助者。God ＿＿＿＿＿＿ those who ＿＿＿＿＿＿ themselves.
5. 誠實為上策。Honesty ＿＿＿＿＿＿ the best policy.
6. 太陽從東方升起。The sun ＿＿＿＿＿＿ in the east.

二、現在進行式：英文裡的現在進行式用來表達「現在正在進行的動作或狀態」。

「現在進行式」的動詞形式： **be 動詞 (am/are/is) + V-ing**

Examples:

1. I <u>am playing</u> volleyball with my classmates.　　（我正在跟同學打排球。）
2. <u>Are</u> many foreigners <u>drinking</u> at the pub now?　（許多老外正在酒吧裡喝酒嗎?）
3. Don't bother Winnie. She <u>is memorizing</u> the English vocabulary.　（不要打擾 Winnie，她正在背英文單字。）

在英文裡，有些動詞不可用進行式，如：have（有）、own（擁有）、like（喜歡）、love（愛）、hate（討厭；恨）、know（知道；認識）、understand（了解）等。這些動詞的共同特點是：它們都不是一個「動作」，而是一種「事實或心理狀態」。

Examples:

1. I <u>have</u> a car. ………（○）　　　2. I'm <u>having</u> a car. ………（✕）

"have" 當「有」時，不可用進行式；但當「吃、喝」之意時，等於 "eat" 或 "drink"，則可以用進行式。

Examples:

1. We <u>are having</u> a big meal. ……（○）　2. We're <u>having</u> a book. ……（✕）

Try This!

根據中文完成英文句子，請用現在進行式作答。

1. Mary 正在房裡彈鋼琴。Mary ＿＿＿＿＿＿ ＿＿＿＿＿＿ the piano in her room.
2. 他們正在討論他們的功課。They ＿＿＿＿＿＿ ＿＿＿＿＿＿ their homework.
3. 請安靜。我現在在跟我老闆講電話。

　　Please be quiet. I ＿＿＿＿＿＿ ＿＿＿＿＿＿ to my boss on the phone now.

三、現在完成式：在英文裡，現在完成式是用來表達「有過的經驗」（中譯為「已經」或「曾經」），或「從過去某時開始，一直持續到現在的動作或狀態」。

「現在完成式」的動詞形式：　**have/has + PP**

Examples:

1. Has he met the girl before?　　　　　　（他以前曾見過這個女生嗎？）
2. I have seen the movie for three times.　（這部電影我已經看過三遍了。）
3. Have you finished the task?　　　　　　（你已完成任務了嗎？）

> 看到句子裡有「for + 一段時間」或「since + 某個過去式的時間或子句」時，主句的動詞會用現在完成式，表示該動作或狀態到目前已持續了多久（for + 一段時間），或該動作、狀態自何時就已開始持續到現在（since + 過去式的時間或子句）。

Examples:

1. We have played basketball for two hours.　（我們已經打了兩個小時的籃球了。）

2. My parents have taken good care of me since I was born.　（我父母從我一出生，就很照顧我。）

3. She has lived in South Africa for 10 years.　（她已經住在南非十年了。）
   = She has lived in South Africa since 10 years ago.
   ⇨表示從十年前，一直到現在，她都住在南非。

選出適當的答案使句意完整。

▢ 1. Fanny and I _____ roommates for four years. We are very close friends.
   (A) are　　　(B) be　　　(C) have been　　　(D) have being

▢ 2. Aaron has studied the new technique _____ five months.
   (A) since　　　(B) for　　　(C) on　　　(D) with

▢ 3. Mary _____ a good dancer _____ she was a child.
   (A) has been; since　(B) is; since　　(C) has been; for　　(D) is; for

當我們在句中看到 "have/has not + PP" 時，中文的意思通常是「還沒…」、「尚未…」，這種句子裡通常可加上 "yet"。

Examples:

1. Kelly has not passed the exam (yet).　　　　　　（Kelly 還沒有通過考試。）
2. We have not eaten breakfast (yet).　　　　　　　（我們還沒吃早餐。）
3. Haven't you finished your homework (yet)?　　　（你還沒做完你的功課嗎？）

表示「去過某地」時，用 "have/has been to..."；表示此人目前已不在該地。
表示「已去某地」時，用 "have/has gone to..."；表示此人目前已在該地。

Examples:

1. Jim has been to Europe before.　　　　　　　　（Jim 以前曾經去過歐洲。）
   ⇨表示 Jim 現在並不在歐洲。
2. We have been to Kenting five times.　　　　　　（我們已經去過墾丁 5 次了。）
   ⇨表示我們現在並不在墾丁。
3. John has gone to Kaohsiung. He won't be back in　（John 已經去高雄了，他下週
   Taipei until next Monday.　　　　　　　　　　一才會回臺北。）
   ⇨表示 John 現在在高雄。

四、現在完成進行式：在英文裡，現在完成進行式是用來表達「從以前某一個時間開始，一直不斷持續到現在的動作或狀態」，這種時態通常可以用來強調動作的持續進行。

「現在完成進行式」的動詞形式：　**have/has + been + V-ing**

Examples:

1. We have been walking for two hours. Let's take a　（我們已經走了兩個小時了。
   rest!　　　　　　　　　　　　　　　　　　　休息一下吧！）

2. My father <u>has been working</u> in the bank for thirty years.

（我父親已經在銀行工作三十年了。）

3. Pinky <u>has been crying</u> all morning.

（Pinky 已經哭了一個早上了。）

4. They <u>have been talking</u> on the phone since three hours ago.

（他們從三小時前，就一直在講電話。）

Try This !

I. 選出適當的答案使句意完整。

☐ 1. Frank _____ never _____ to the U.S.

　(A) is; been 　　(B) has; being 　　(C) has; be 　　(D) has; been

☐ 2. You _____ me too many questions. I'm beginning to feel tired.

　(A) have asked 　　　　　　(B) are asked

　(C) have been asked 　　　　(D) asks

☐ 3. Lisa _____ Italy. She is not in Taiwan now.

　(A) has been to 　(B) has gone to 　(C) is going to 　(D) will go to

☐ 4. I am afraid that I can't go to the movie with you tonight. I _____ finished my report yet.

　(A) have 　　(B) haven't 　　(C) have been 　　(D) haven't been

☐ 5. The boss _____ Germany this morning. He is not able to meet you within this week.

　(A) has gone to 　(B) hasn't gone 　(C) have been 　(D) haven't been

II. 根據中文完成英文句子。

1. 你已經打了一整天的電動了。立刻把電腦關掉！

You _____ been _____ the computer game the whole day. Turn off the computer right now!

2. 我女兒還沒打電話給我，我很擔心。

I am worried that my daughter _____ called me _____.

3. 我以前曾經看過這個電影明星。

I _____ _____ the movie star before.

4. 我的女友已經去美國進修了。

My girlfriend _____ _____ _____ America for further study.

2–3 　過去式

一、過去簡單式：在英文裡，過去簡單式是用來表示「過去的事實、狀態、習慣或動作」。

「過去簡單式」的動詞形式	be 動詞	"was"（主詞為第一、三人稱單數或單數名詞）；"were"（主詞為第二人稱、複數名詞）。
	一般動詞	過去式動詞。
	助動詞	過去式助動詞和一般動詞連用於「否定句」或「疑問句」，且助動詞後的動詞一律用原形。

<< 表示過去的事實或狀態 >>

Examples:

1. Mia <u>was</u> in Taiwan five years ago. 　　　　（Mia 五年前在臺灣。）

2. <u>Were</u> you at home last night? 　　　　（你昨晚在家嗎？）

3. The twins <u>were</u> fat and cute when they <u>were</u> little children. 　　（這對雙胞胎小時候又胖又可愛。）

<< 表示過去的習慣或動作 >>

Examples:

1. Sue <u>got</u> a high grade in biology yesterday. 　（Sue 昨天生物考得很好。）

2. They <u>studied</u> psychology in the U.S. before. 　（他們以前在美國唸心理學。）

3. Allen <u>walked</u> into the classroom, <u>sat</u> down on the chair, and <u>started</u> to read comic books. 　（Allen 走進教室，坐在椅子上，然後開始看漫畫。）

4. They usually <u>listened</u> to pop music together when they <u>were</u> in high school. 　（他們在高中時常常一起聽流行樂。）

在英文裡，"just now" 是「剛才」的意思，所以句子裡的動詞要用過去式。

Examples:

1. Michael <u>had</u> his dinner just now.　　　　（Michael 剛才吃過晚餐。）

2. He <u>sang</u> a song for us just now.　　　　（他剛才唱了一首歌給我們聽。）

表示「過去的習慣」，英文可用 "used to + 原形 V"。

Examples:

1. We <u>used to take</u> a walk in the morning.　　（我們過去習慣在早上散步。）

2. Sandy <u>used to have</u> a glass of milk before she went to bed.　　（Sandy 過去習慣在睡前喝一杯牛奶。）

<< 過去式助動詞常用於否定句或疑問句 >>

Examples:

1. We <u>didn't know</u> each other when we were young.　（我們年輕時並不認識彼此。）

2. <u>Did</u> you <u>help</u> the old lady yesterday?　　（你昨天有幫那位老太太嗎？）

根據中文完成英文句子。

1. 你昨天晚餐之後有吃藥嗎？

　　_____ you _____ the medicine after dinner yesterday?

2. 我以前習慣早起。

　　I _____ _____ _____ up early.

3. Sara 剛才在麥當勞吃了一個大漢堡。

　　Sara _____ a big hamburger at McDonald's just _____.

4. 昨天晚上有下雨嗎？_____ it _____ last night?

5. 他堅持他沒有犯任何錯誤。

　　He insisted that he _____ _____ any mistake.

6. 我同事和我去年夏天去蘇格蘭。

　　My colleagues and I _____ to Scotland last summer.

二、**過去進行式**：在英文裡，過去進行式是用來表達「過去某個時間正在進行的動作」。

「過去進行式」的動詞形式： **be 動詞 (was/were) + V-ing**

◯**E**xamples:

1. I <u>was playing</u> basketball at noon yesterday. （我昨天正午時正在打籃球。）

2. <u>Were</u> the students <u>eating</u> snacks at three o'clock yesterday afternoon? （昨天下午三點時學生在吃零嘴嗎？）

常見句型 1：<u>S + was/were + V-ing</u> + <u>when + 過去式子句</u>
　　　　　 = <u>When + 過去式子句</u>，<u>S + was/were + V-ing</u>

◯**E**xample:

It <u>was raining</u> heavily <u>when *I arrived in Taipei last night*</u>.
= <u>When I arrived in Taipei last night</u>, it <u>was raining</u> heavily.
（我昨天晚上到臺北時，正在下大雨。）

常見句型 2：<u>S₁ + was/were + V₁-ing</u> + <u>while + S₂ + was/were + V₂-ing</u>
　　　　　 = <u>While + S₂ + was/were + V₂-ing</u>, <u>S₁+ was/were + V₁-ing</u>

◯**E**xample:

You <u>were playing</u> video games <u>while *your sister* was doing *her homework*</u>.
= <u>While *your sister* was doing *her homework*</u>, you <u>were playing</u> video games.
（你妹妹在做功課時，你在打電動。）

根據中文完成英文句子。

1. 當我到家時，電話鈴聲正在響。

　　_____ I _____ home, the telephone was _____.

2. 我在唱歌時，她在跳舞。

　　I _____ _____ while she _____ _____.

三、過去完成式： 在英文裡，過去完成式是用來表達「過去某個動作或過去某個時間之前就已完成的動作或已存在的狀況」，也就是比過去某個動作或過去某個時間之前更早發生的動作或狀況；中文的意思是「已經」或「曾經」。

「**過去完成式**」的動詞形式：　**had + PP**

Examples:

1. I <u>had finished</u> my report before I <u>went</u> to bed last night.

   （昨晚上床睡覺前，我就已經完成報告。）

   ⇨ 「昨晚上床睡覺前」代表在過去某個動作之前，故主句動詞用過去完成式。

2. They <u>had bought</u> the house the year before.

   （他們去年就已經買下了這棟房子。）

   ⇨ 「去年」代表過去的時間之前，故主句動詞用過去完成式。

句子裡若有兩個過去發生的動作時，先發生的用過去完成式，後發生的用過去簡單式。

Examples:

1. Edison <u>said</u> that he <u>had seen</u> May once.

   （Edison 說他曾經看過 May 一次。）

   ⇨ 「Edison 看過 May」比「Edison 說」先發生，所以「看」用過去完成式，「說」用過去簡單式。

2. I <u>found</u> the cell phone that I <u>had lost</u> last week.

   （我找到我上週弄丟的手機了。）

   ⇨ 「我弄丟手機」比「我找到」先發生，所以「弄丟」用過去完成式，「找到」用過去簡單式。

選出適當的答案使句意完整。

1. She said that she _____ a tiger.

   (A) has never seen　(B) had seeing　(C) had never seen　(D) had been seen

2. He _____ the pictures of the girl several times before he met her.

   (A) saw　　(B) has seen　　(C) had been seen　(D) had seen

四、過去完成進行式：在英文裡，「過去完成進行式」的用法大致上與「過去完成式」相同，只是前者通常可以用來強調動作的持續進行。

「過去完成進行式」的動詞形式： **had + been + V-ing**

Examples:

1. The nurse <u>had been working</u> very hard all day; she was exhausted after work.
（這位護士辛苦工作了整天，下班後就累垮了。）

2. He <u>had been waiting for</u> Vivian for an hour before she showed up.
（在 Vivian 出現前，他已經等了一小時。）

3. Before the mother came home, the kid <u>had been playing</u> for three hours.
（在媽媽回到家之前，這個小孩已經玩了三小時。）

I. 選出適當的答案使句意完整。

☐ 1. Tina _____ the piano for an hour before her mom came back.
    (A) has played   (B) has been playing
    (C) had been played   (D) had been playing

☐ 2. Before Joy's parents came home, she _____ dinner for two hours.
    (A) has prepared   (B) has been preparing
    (C) had been prepared   (D) had been preparing

II. 根據中文完成英文句子，請以過去進行式、過去完成式或過去完成進行式作答。

1. 客廳很吵，我哥哥和他的朋友正在舉辦派對。

   It was very noisy in the living room. My brother and his friends _____ _____ a party.

2. 當旅程結束時，妻子和我都很疲倦，我們已持續旅行超過一個月了。

   My wife and I were very tired at the end of the journey. We _____ _____ _____ for more than one month.

3. 當我去探望她時，她已經病了三天。

   She _____ _____ ill for three days when I visited her.

2-4　未來式

一、未來簡單式：在英文裡，未來簡單式是用來表示「未來要發生的動作或狀態」。

「未來簡單式」的動詞形式： **will + 原形動詞**

Examples:

1. I <u>will move</u> into my new apartment next week. （我下禮拜要搬進我的新公寓。）
2. <u>Will</u> he <u>realize</u> his dream of becoming a painter? （他會實現成為畫家的夢想嗎？）
3. According to the weather report, it <u>will not/won't</u> <u>rain</u> tonight. （根據氣象報告，今晚不會下雨。）

在英文裡，表示「即將」或是「短時間之內」將發生的動作，可以用 "be going to + 原形動詞" 或 "be about to + 原形動詞" 來代替 "will + 原形動詞"；有時候，甚至可用現在進行式 "be + V-ing" 代替 "will + 原形動詞"，表示即將發生的動作或狀態。

Examples:

1. We <u>are going to</u> take the exam next week. （我們下週將要應試。）
2. I <u>am about to</u> move into the dormitory next week. （我下禮拜要搬進宿舍。）
3. He <u>is visiting</u> us in an hour. （他一小時內會來拜訪我們。）

根據中文完成英文句子。

1. Betty 未來會成為一位老師嗎？

　　_____ Betty _____ a teacher in the future?

2. 我叔叔明天要從夏威夷回來了。

　　My uncle is _____ back from Hawaii tomorrow.

3. 你下午要做什麼？What are you _____ to _____ in the afternoon?

> "There will be + N...." 的句型表示「將有…」；
> "There will not/won't be + N...." 的句型表示「將沒有…」。

Examples:

1. There will not/won't be any winner or loser in the battle. （這場戰役中，將不會有任何贏家或輸家。）

2. Will there be an English quiz tomorrow morning? （明天早上會有英文小考嗎？）

二、未來進行式： 在英文裡，未來進行式是用來表達「未來某個時間將在進行的動作」。

「未來進行式」的動詞形式： **will + be + V-ing**

Examples:

1. I will be having my dinner at 7 o'clock tonight. （今晚七點，我將在吃晚餐。）

2. The students will be taking the weekly math test at 7:30 tomorrow morning. （明天早上七點半，學生們將在考數學週考。）

Try This!

I. 選出正確的答案。

☐ 1. There _____ an exciting basketball game in NTU next month.
   (A) will be   (B) has   (C) will have   (D) is being

☐ 2. Grace _____ her piano lesson at five o'clock tomorrow evening.
   (A) will be take   (B) will be taking
   (C) takes   (D) is going to taking

☐ 3. What _____ the teacher _____ if she finds out what we have done?
   (A) is, do   (B) will, to do   (C) is, about do   (D) will, do

II. 根據中文完成英文句子。

1. 未來將會有很多機器人。

   _____ _____ _____ a lot of robots in the future.

2. 明天早上五點，我將在慢跑。

   I _____ _____ _____ at 5 o'clock tomorrow morning.

三、未來完成式：在英文裡，未來完成式是用來表達「未來某個動作或某個時間之前將已完成的動作或狀況」，也就是比未來某個動作或某個時間之前更早發生的動作或狀況；中文的意思是「將已…」。

「未來完成式」的動詞形式： **will + have + PP**

Example:

1. I will have moved into my new apartment before the end of this month.

（這個月底前，我將已經搬進我的新公寓了。）

2. If Rachel arrives there too late, her idol will have left the concert.

   ⇨ 表時間或條件的副詞子句中未來的動作要用現在式 **(arrives)** 表示。

（如果 Rachel 太晚到那裡，她的偶像將已經離開演唱會。）

四、未來完成進行式：在英文裡，「未來完成進行式」的用法大致上與「未來完成式」相同，只是前者通常可以用來強調動作的持續進行。

「未來完成進行式」的動詞形式： **will + have + been + V-ing**

Example:

By June, I will have been working in the U.S. for two years.

（到六月，我將已經在美國工作兩年了。）

根據中文完成英文句子。

1. 在他明年回臺灣前，我們將已蓋好這棟大房子。

   Before he ＿＿＿＿＿＿ back to Taiwan next year, we ＿＿＿＿＿＿ ＿＿＿＿＿＿ ＿＿＿＿＿＿ the big house.

2. 當他來幫我們時，我們將已經工作三小時了。

   We ＿＿＿＿＿＿ ＿＿＿＿＿＿ ＿＿＿＿＿＿ ＿＿＿＿＿＿ for three hours when he ＿＿＿＿＿＿ to our help.

☑ Test & Review

I. 選出正確的答案。

☐ 1. _____ you _____ the meaning of true love?

    (A) Does, understand   (B) Are, understanding

    (C) Have, understanding   (D) Do, understand

☐ 2. Kim _____ to school every day.

    (A) walks   (B) is walking   (C) has walked   (D) walk

☐ 3. The students _____ their lunch in the classroom right now.

    (A) eating   (B) are having   (C) have   (D) will eat

☐ 4. We _____ a car before we _____ a house.

    (A) had bought, had bought   (B) bought, bought

    (C) had bought, bought   (D) have bought, bought

☐ 5. When Sally's mom _____ back home from work, Sally will _____ studying English for three hours.

    (A) comes, have been   (B) will come, have been

    (C) comes, be   (D) will come, be

☐ 6. I _____ interested in Egypt _____ I was a child.

    (A) was, since   (B) am, for

    (C) have been, since   (D) have been, when

☐ 7. When Jenny walked into the pub, all her friends _____.

    (A) laughed and drank   (B) were laughing and drinking

    (C) were laughing and drank   (D) laughed and drinking

☐ 8. Before Sophia decided to move to Mainland China, she _____ a job there.

    (A) found   (B) was finding   (C) will find   (D) had found

☐ 9. Stanley _____ for the final exam while Jerry _____ the net.

    (A) prepared, surfed   (B) was preparing, was surfing

    (C) was preparing, surfing   (D) prepared, was surfing

☐ 10. _____ you ever _____ to Africa?

    (A) Do, be   (B) Have, went   (C) Have, gone   (D) Have, been

II. 根據中文完成英文句子。

11. 當我昨天回家時，我媽媽早已經在準備晚餐了。

When I _____ home yesterday, my mom _____ _____ _____ dinner.

12. 只要你用功讀書，你明年就會進入一所好大學。

As long as you _____ hard, you _____ _____ a good university next year.

13. Jessica 已經去香港了。她現在不在臺灣。

Jessica _____ _____ _____ Hong Kong. She is not in Taiwan now.

III. 選出正確答案以完成句子。

14. While Anne was talking to Gilbert, _____.

15. Before the general manager walked into the meeting room, _____.

16. What will you do _____?

17. If we don't protect our environment, _____.

18. Amanda and Mandy were watching TV _____.

19. Rita doesn't know much about Cambodia _____.

20. You can't find Sally here _____.

(A) because she has gone to Hua-lian
(B) we will end up with no clean water to drink
(C) his secretary had prepared all the information he needed for him
(D) when their parents walked into the living room
(E) Diana was overhearing what they were saying
(F) when your neighbors make lots of noise late at night
(G) because she has never been there

3-1 被動語態的意義、原則與形式

在英文裡,語態分為「主動語態」(active voice) 和「被動語態」(passive voice) 兩種。主動語態的主詞為「主動」做某個動作的名詞或代名詞,而被動語態的主詞則為「承受動作者」。

主動語態	被動語態
S + V+ O	S + be 動詞 + PP (+ by N)
David stole the money. (David 偷了錢。)	The money was stolen by David. (錢被 David 偷了。)

被動語態的動詞形式: **be 動詞 + PP**

Examples:

1. The window <u>was broken</u> last night.　　　　　　(昨天晚上窗戶被打破了。)
   ⇨窗戶是「被」打破的,故動詞用 be 動詞 + PP。

2. The wounded soldiers <u>are sent</u> to the hospital.　(受傷的士兵被送到醫院。)
   ⇨受傷的士兵是「被」送到醫院的,故動詞用 be 動詞 + PP。

> 有時候在中文的句子裡,並沒有「被…」的意思出現,但是在英文裡,只要句子有「被動」的含意,動詞一律都要用被動語態。

Examples:

1. The game <u>was held</u> in the school last Friday.　　(比賽於上週五在學校舉行。)
   ⇨比賽是「被」舉行的,故動詞用 be 動詞 + PP。

2. English <u>is spoken</u> in many countries in the world.　(世界上許多國家說英語。)
   ⇨英語是「被」說的,故動詞用 be 動詞 + PP。

> 當做出動作者的身分不明確、不重要或眾所皆知時,用被動語態較合適,且 by N 常可省略。

Examples:

1. The window <u>was broken</u> (by somebody) last night.
   ⇨被誰打破的,根本沒人知道(不明確),故不用寫出。

2. English is spoken (by people) in many countries in the world.

⇨英語是被「人」說的，不重要且眾所皆知，故也不用寫出。

3-2 主動語態改被動語態

英文裡，只要有受詞的主動語態句子幾乎都能改寫為被動語態。原則如下：

> 1. 把原受詞提到句首當主詞。
> 2. 把原主詞放到 by 後面形成介系詞片語。

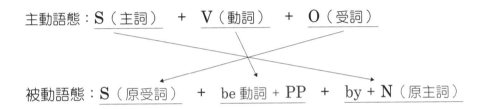

主動語態：S（主詞） + V（動詞） + O（受詞）

被動語態：S（原受詞） + be 動詞 + PP + by + N（原主詞）

Examples:

1. Tim wrote two letters last night.　（Tim 昨天晚上寫了兩封信。）
   ⇨ Two letters were written by Tim last night.

2. My boyfriend loves me deeply.　（我男朋友深深地愛著我。）
   ⇨ I am loved deeply by my boyfriend.

3. Many people speak Taiwanese in Taiwan.　（在臺灣很多人說臺語。）
   ⇨ Taiwanese is spoken by many people in Taiwan.

4. Our school will hold the final exam next week.　（我們學校將在下禮拜舉行期末考。）
   ⇨ The final exam will be held by our school next week.

根據中文句意及提示字完成下列句子。
1. 這個工作上禮拜完成 (*finish*) 了。The job ＿＿＿＿＿＿ ＿＿＿＿＿＿ last week.
2. 我的衣服被偷 (*steal*) 了。My clothes ＿＿＿＿＿ ＿＿＿＿＿.

3-3　被動語態的時態

任何時態的被動語態，動詞都是用「be 動詞 + PP」，但至於用何種形式的 be 動詞，就要視每個句子中不同的時態來決定。

	現　在	過　去	未　來
簡單式	am/are/is + PP	was/were + PP	will be + PP
進行式	am/are/is + being + PP	was/were + being + PP	
完成式	have/has + been + PP	had + been + PP	will have been + PP

一、現在簡單式的被動語態：　**S + am/are/is + PP**

Examples:

1. Mary <u>helps</u> the poor boy.　　　　　　　　（Mary 幫助那個可憐的男孩。）
   ⇒ The poor boy <u>is helped</u> by Mary.

2. Many young people <u>learn</u> English and Japanese.　（許多年輕人學習英文和日文。）
   ⇒ English and Japanese <u>are learned</u> by many young people.

二、過去簡單式的被動語態：　**S + was/were + PP**

Examples:

1. Many young people <u>liked</u> Madonna and Celine Dion ten years ago.　　　　　（十年前，許多年輕人喜歡 Madonna 和 Celine Dion。）
   ⇒ Madonna and Celine Dion <u>were liked</u> by many young people ten years ago.

2. Mark Twain <u>wrote</u> the famous novel "The Adventures of Tom Sawyer."　　　（馬克·吐溫寫了《湯姆歷險記》這本有名的小說。）

⇨ The famous novel "The Adventures of Tom Sawyer" <u>was written</u> by Mark Twain.

三、未來簡單式的被動語態： S + will be + PP

Examples:

1. The teacher <u>will announce</u> the result of the competition tomorrow.　　（老師明天將公布競賽結果。）
   ⇨ The result of the competition <u>will be announced</u> by the teacher tomorrow.

2. Tom <u>will give</u> a speech in class today.　　（Tom 今天會在課堂上發表演說。）
   ⇨ A speech <u>will be given</u> in class by Tom today.

Try This!

I. 選出正確的答案。

☐ 1. The thief _____ by the police last month.
   (A) caught　　　(B) is catching　　(C) was caught　　(D) will be caught

☐ 2. The basketball game _____ by our school every year.
   (A) is held　　　(B) will be held　　(C) is holding　　(D) was holding

☐ 3. I believe that a time machine _____ in the near future.
   (A) is invented　(B) will invent　　(C) is inventing　(D) will be invented

☐ 4. I _____ by my teacher every day for being late for school.
   (A) am punished　(B) am punishing　(C) punished　　(D) was punishing

☐ 5. These pop singers _____ taking drugs at a pub last night.
   (A) were found　　(B) were finding　(C) will be found　(D) are found

II. 根據中文完成英文句子。

1. 他的信用卡昨天被偷了。
   His credit card _____ _____ yesterday.

2. 這個罪犯有天將受到嚴厲的懲罰。
   The criminal _____ _____ punished severely someday.

3. 我妹妹不常被邀請去派對。她太害羞了。
   My sister _____ often _____ to parties; she is too shy.

四、現在進行式的被動語態： S + am/are/is + being + PP

Examples:

1. My dad <u>is telling</u> me a story. （我爸爸正在跟我說一個故事。）
   ⇨ I <u>am being told</u> a story by my dad.

2. Miss Hsu <u>is teaching</u> the students the history of China. （徐老師正在教學生中國歷史。）
   ⇨ The students <u>are being taught</u> the history of China by Miss Hsu.

五、過去進行式的被動語態： S + was/were + being + PP

Examples:

1. They <u>were playing</u> computer games at 10:00 yesterday morning. （他們昨天早上十點正在打電動。）
   ⇨ Computer games <u>were being played</u> by them at 10:00 yesterday morning.

2. Joe <u>was using</u> the computer at 11:00 last night. （Joe 昨晚十一點時正在用電腦。）
   ⇨ The computer <u>was being used</u> by Joe at 11:00 last night.

根據中文及提示字完成英文句子。

1. 這些犯人現在正在接受警察的訊問 (question)。
   These criminals ＿＿＿＿＿ ＿＿＿＿＿ ＿＿＿＿＿ by the police now.
2. John 昨天早上八點正在洗襪子。
   The socks ＿＿＿＿＿ ＿＿＿＿＿ ＿＿＿＿＿ by John at 8:00 a.m. yesterday.
3. 我媽媽正在責備我。I ＿＿＿＿＿ ＿＿＿＿＿ ＿＿＿＿＿ by my mom.

六、現在完成式的被動語態： **S + have/has + been + PP**

Examples:

1. Terry <u>has bought</u> many dictionaries.
   ⇒ Many dictionaries <u>have been bought</u> by Terry.

   （Terry 已經買了許多字典。）

2. We <u>have got hooked on</u> this novel.
   ⇒ This novel <u>has been got hooked on</u> by us.

   （我們已經迷上這本小說了。）

七、過去完成式的被動語態： **S + had + been + PP**

Example:

The room was clean because Tom <u>had cleaned</u> it.
⇒ The room was clean because it <u>had been cleaned</u>
by Tom.

（房間乾淨是因為 Tom 之前已經清理過了。）

八、未來完成式的被動語態： **S + will + have + been + PP**

Example:

The teacher <u>will have announced</u> the result of the
exam by Sunday.
⇒ The result of the exam <u>will have been announced</u>
by the teacher by Sunday.

（週日前，老師將已公布考試的結果了。）

根據中文完成英文句子。

1. 這部電影我已經看過三遍了。
   The movie ＿＿＿＿＿＿ ＿＿＿＿＿＿ ＿＿＿＿＿＿ three times by me.
2. 在你回到家之前，電視將已經修好了。The TV set ＿＿＿＿＿＿ ＿＿＿＿＿＿
   ＿＿＿＿＿＿ ＿＿＿＿＿＿ before you come home.
3. 在 Joe 決定買這場音樂會的門票前，票已經賣光了。
   All tickets to this concert ＿＿＿＿＿＿ ＿＿＿＿＿＿ ＿＿＿＿＿＿ before Joe
   decided to buy one.

3-4　含「助動詞」或「感官動詞」的被動語態

一、含助動詞的被動語態

當句子裡含「助動詞」，改為被動語態時仍要維持相同的助動詞。

Examples:

1. We <u>must finish</u> the report today.　　　　　（我們今天必須完成報告。）
   ⇨ The report <u>must be finished</u> by us today.
2. They <u>should send</u> the sick to the hospital as soon　（他們應該盡快把病人送到醫
   as possible.　　　　　　　　　　　　　　　　院。）
   ⇨ The sick <u>should be sent</u> to the hospital by them
   as soon as possible.

二、含感官動詞的被動語態

當句子裡有「感官動詞」時，改為被動語態的公式為：

> **S + be** 動詞 **+** 感官動詞 **(watched/seen/heard/felt) + to +** 原形動詞

Examples:

1. I often <u>see</u> my brother <u>surf</u> the net at night.　（我常看見我弟弟晚上上網。）
   ⇨ My brother <u>is</u> often <u>seen to surf</u> the net at
   night by me.

> 如果感官動詞後面接的是現在分詞，改為被動語態時就直接沿用現在分詞。例如 I saw my brother surfing the net that night. → My brother was seen surfing the net that night.。

將下列句子改寫為被動語態的句子。

1. Will you wash your dirty clothes tomorrow?
   ⇨ _____
2. I saw a strange man with a gun going into the president's residence.
   ⇨ _____

3–5 「疑問句」、「祈使句」及「否定句」的被動語態

一、Do/Does/Did 開頭的疑問句改被動語態

改寫原則：

> 1. 原受詞提到前面當主詞。
> 2. 原主詞放到 by 後面形成介系詞片語。

主動語態： Do/Does/Did + S（主詞） + 原形 V + O（受詞）？

被動語態：be 動詞 + S（原受詞） + PP + by + N（原主詞）？

Examples:

1. Do you eat at least an egg every day?　　　　（你每天都至少吃一個蛋嗎？）

   ⇒ Is at least an egg eaten by you every day?

   【簡單現在式，且新主詞為單數 "an egg"，故被動語態的 be 動詞用 "is"。】

2. Did they feed the kitten yesterday?　　　　（他們昨天有餵這隻小貓嗎？）

   ⇒ Was the kitten fed by them yesterday?

   【簡單過去式，且新主詞為單數 "the kitten"，故被動語態的 be 動詞用 "was"。】

3. Did your sister sing those songs in the karaoke club?　（妳妹妹在卡拉 OK 唱了那些

   ⇒ Were those songs sung by your sister in the　歌嗎？）

   karaoke club?

   【簡單過去式，且新主詞為複數 "those songs"，故被動語態的 be 動詞用 "were"。】

將下列句子改寫為被動語態。

1. Did Peggy wash the car last week?

   ⇒_____

2. Did you break this vase?

   ⇒_____

二、疑問詞開頭的疑問句改被動語態

疑問詞 (Where/When/Why/Which/How) 開頭的疑問句改被動語態時，仍然要保留疑問詞在句首，再視句子的時態及新主詞的單複數來決定 be 動詞的形式。

Examples:

1. Where <u>do</u> they <u>play</u> hide-and-seek?　　　　　　（他們在哪裡玩捉迷藏？）
   ⇨ Where <u>is</u> hide-and-seek <u>played</u> by them?

   【簡單現在式，且新主詞為單數 "hide-and-seek"，故被動語態的 be 動詞用 "is"。】

2. When <u>did</u> Sue <u>buy</u> these shoes?　　　　　　（Sue 什麼時候買這些鞋子的？）
   ⇨ When <u>were</u> these shoes <u>bought</u> by Sue?

   【簡單過去式，且新主詞為複數 "these shoes"，故被動語態的 be 動詞用 "were"。】

3. How <u>will</u> he <u>win</u> a role in the film?　　　　　（他要如何獲得那部電影中的角
   ⇨ How <u>will</u> a role in the film <u>be won</u> by him?　色？）

   【簡單未來式 "will" 的疑問句，故被動語態的動詞用 "will be + PP"。】

三、Who 開頭的疑問句改被動語態

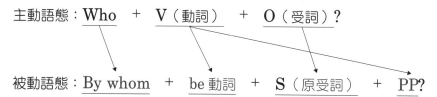

主動語態：Who ＋ V（動詞）＋ O（受詞）?

被動語態：By whom ＋ be 動詞 ＋ S（原受詞）＋ PP?

Examples:

1. Who <u>ate</u> my favorite cookies?　　　　　　（誰吃了我最愛的餅乾？）
   ⇨ <u>By whom</u> <u>were</u> my favorite cookies <u>eaten</u>?

2. Who <u>bought</u> this book?　　　　　　（誰買了這本書？）
   ⇨ <u>By whom</u> <u>was</u> this book <u>bought</u>?

將下列句子改寫為被動語態的句子。

1. Where should little Johnny put the toys? ⇨＿＿＿＿＿＿＿＿＿＿
2. Who taught you English? ⇨＿＿＿＿＿＿＿＿＿＿

四、祈使句的被動語態

肯定	Let + O（受詞）+ be 動詞 + PP
否定	Don't let + O（受詞）+ be 動詞 + PP

Examples:

1. Open the door.（肯定祈使句）　　　　　　　　（把門打開。）
   ⇨ Let the door be opened.
2. Don't break the rules.（否定祈使句）　　　　　（不要違反規定。）
   ⇨ Don't let the rules be broken.

五、否定句的被動語態

　　否定句的被動語態很簡單，不論是何種時態，只要在助動詞後面加上 "not" 即可。

Examples:

1. The chair was not made by this man.　　　（這張椅子不是這個男人製作的。）
2. The report has not been finished.　　　　　（報告還沒有完成。）
3. Pornography should not be brought into campus.　（色情書刊不該被帶進校園。）
4. Is this desk not made of wood?　　　　　（這張書桌不是用木頭做的嗎？）

 **Try This !**

將下列句子改寫為被動語態的句子。

1. Ring the doorbell.
   ⇨ _____

2. Alice didn't see Joe playing baseball this afternoon.
   ⇨ _____

☑Test & Review

I. 選出正確的答案。

1. Frank _____ by a motorcycle yesterday, but fortunately he was not seriously injured.

   (A) is hit   (B) was hitting   (C) hit   (D) was hit

2. When you come home tomorrow evening, the feast _____ well prepared.

   (A) will have been   (B) will have being (C) will   (D) is

3. What is done can not _____.

   (A) be done   (B) be undone   (C) be doing   (D) do

4. German _____ in many European countries.

   (A) is spoken   (B) speaks   (C) is speaking   (D) will speak

5. _____ was the fish poisoned?

   (A) Whom   (B) What   (C) By whom   (D) With whom

6. When will the goods _____ to us by the mail-order company?

   (A) be sent   (B) send   (C) be sending   (D) being sent

7. Shelly was seen _____ the guitar after school yesterday.

   (A) played   (B) play   (C) to play   (D) be played

8. Let the window _____.

   (A) to be opened   (B) open   (C) be opening   (D) be opened

II. 依據中文完成英文句子。

9. 甘迺迪總統是被誰射殺 (shoot) 的？

   _____ _____ was President Kennedy _____?

10. 這個狡猾的嫌疑犯不會被警方抓到的。

    The sly suspect will _____ _____ _____ by the police.

11. Kay 的生日舞會什麼時候舉行？

    When will Kay's birthday party _____ _____?

12. 我們昨天看到 Sheri 放學後在教室彈吉他。

    Sheri _____ _____ _____ _____ the guitar in the classroom after school yesterday.

13. 這些廢水要怎麼處理？

_____ will the waste water _____ handled?

14. 歐洲各地都使用歐元嗎？

_____ Euro _____ everywhere in Europe?

15. 我的電腦還沒有修好。

My computer _____ not _____ _____ yet.

III. 將下列句子改寫為被動語態。

16. Don't turn off the light when I am reading.

   ⇨ _____

17. Someone left a note on my desk.

   ⇨ _____

18. Has Jim taken the medicine?

   ⇨ _____

19. Jordan's fans called him "Air Jordan."

   ⇨ _____

20. Finish the homework at once.

   ⇨ _____

21. My students are recycling the waste paper.

   ⇨ _____

22. They will not give up the rare opportunity.

   ⇨ _____

23. Why did David throw away the toy robot?

   ⇨ _____

24. Mary heard her sister crying in her room.

   ⇨ _____

25. Who invented cars?

   ⇨ _____

助動詞的功用在於輔助動詞形成疑問句、否定句，或者表達說話者的語氣或態度等，可分為純助動詞與情態助動詞兩種。

4-1　純助動詞

除了 do、does、did 以外，完成式的 have、has、had 以及進行式和被動語態中的 be 動詞也歸類為純助動詞。

一、助動詞的「否定句」句型

(1) S + do/does/did + not + V　　Sally <u>doesn't understand</u> your explanation.
　　（Sally 不懂你的解釋。）
(2) S + be 動詞 + not + V-ing/PP　The game <u>wasn't held</u> on Saturday.
　　（比賽不在週六舉行。）
(3) S + have/has/had + not + PP　John <u>hasn't been</u> to Korea.
　　（John 還沒去過韓國。）

二、助動詞的「疑問句」句型

(1) Do/Does/Did + S + V?　　<u>Did</u> Mark <u>take</u> away my umbrella?
　　（Mark 拿走我的雨傘嗎？）
(2) Be 動詞 + S + V-ing/PP?　<u>Are</u> you <u>listening</u> to me?
　　（你有在聽我說話嗎？）
(3) Have/Has/Had + S + PP?　<u>Has</u> he <u>left</u>?
　　（他已經離開了嗎？）

三、助動詞的「替代作用」（代替前面提過的動詞）

(1) Yes, S + do/does/did/have/has/ 　　had/be 動詞	<u>Does</u> she <u>like</u> jogging? Yes, she <u>does</u>. （她喜歡慢跑嗎？是的，她喜歡。）
(2) No, S + do/does/did/have/has/ 　　had/be 動詞 + not	<u>Do</u> you <u>know</u> Annie? No, I <u>don't</u>. （你認識 Annie 嗎？不，我不認識。）
(3) So + do/does/did/have/has/had/ 　　be 動詞 + S	John <u>enjoyed</u> the concert last night. So <u>did</u> I. （John 很享受昨天的演唱會，我也是。）
(4) Neither + do/does/did/have/has/ 　　had/be 動詞 + S neither 本身已經帶有否定意味，故不加 not。	Peter <u>hasn't done</u> the work. Neither <u>has</u> Yvonne. （Peter 還沒完成工作，Yvonne 也還沒。）

四、助動詞的「加強語氣」用法

S + do/does/did + V	Linda <u>does teach</u> in that famous high school. （Linda 的確在那間著名的中學教書。）

Try This!

I. 將下列句子畫線部分改寫為含有「So + 助動詞 +S」或「Neither + 助動詞 + S」的句子。

1. Mary has had her lunch. <u>I have had my lunch, too.</u>

_____

2. Elsa didn't take away the cake. <u>George didn't take away the cake, either.</u>

_____

3. Johnson isn't a cook. <u>Tim isn't a cook, either.</u>

_____

II. 根據中文完成英文句子。

1. 他說他沒有拿我的娃娃，但我確定他有。

He said that he _____ take my doll, but I was sure he _____.

2. Peter 的確有出席會議，只是你沒有看到他。

Peter _____ attend the meeting, but you didn't see him.

4–2 情態助動詞

情態助動詞可以用來表達很多意思，如建議、義務、推測、萬一、允許、請求、能力等等的意思。情態助動詞的基本特點如下：

(1) 情態助動詞的基本句型：

> S + 情態助動詞 + 原形動詞

(2) 情態助動詞不受時態影響變化，could、should、would、might 不見得只能用在過去式，will 也不一定只能用在未來式，彈性很大。

一、should

> should 可以表達包括建議、義務、推測、萬一等意思。

Examples:

<< 建議 >>　You should use the Internet to learn English.
　　　　　　（你應該利用網際網路來學英文。）

<< 義務 >>　Students should hand in their homework on time.
　　　　　　（學生應該準時交作業。）

<< 推測 >>　He has been working hard, so he should be promoted.
　　　　　　（他一直工作得很賣力，所以他應該會升官。）

<< 萬一 >>　If Karen should come, tell her to wait for me.
　　　　　　（萬一 Karen 來了，請她稍等我一下。）

> should 表達「該做而沒有做的事」的句型：
> (1) S + should have PP + ... ⇨「過去該做卻沒有做的事」
> (2) S + should not have PP + ... ⇨「過去不該做卻做了的事」

Examples:

1. Hector should have studied hard yesterday.　　（Hector 昨天應該用功的。）
2. You shouldn't have stayed overnight in the hotel last night.　　（你昨晚不該在飯店過夜的。）

二、will

will 除了表示未來外，也可以表示意志或請求的意思。

Examples:

<< 未來 >>   I will soon be able to read French.   （我很快就會讀法文了。）

<< 意志 >>   They will lend us some money.   （他們願意借我們一些錢。）

<< 請求 >>   Will you do me a favor?   （能麻煩你幫我一下嗎？）

Try This !

I. 填入適當的情態助動詞 should (shouldn't) 或 will 使句意完整。

1. _____ you give me a piece of paper to write on?

2. You _____ have gone to bed early last night. Then, you wouldn't fall asleep in class today.

3. She _____ have done such a stupid thing.

4. Tell me the truth, or I _____ not talk to you any more.

5. You _____ stop smoking. It's not good for your health.

6. _____ you go to the concert with me? I have some free tickets.

7. Don't worry about her. She _____ overcome the loss of her daughter.

II. 根據中文完成英文句子。

1. 你不應該把她的書丟到垃圾桶裡的。

   You _____ _____ _____ her books into the trash can.

2. 幫我把箱子搬到外面好嗎？

   _____ you _____ the box outside for me?

三、can & could

can 與 could 可以表達能力、可能性、許可等意義，與其他情態助動詞比較不同的地方是，當表達能力時，can 用在現在的情況，could 則用在過去的情況。

Examples:

<< 能力 >>　1. I can't speak Spanish.　　　　（我不會說西班牙文。）
　　　　　　2. She could swim when she was　（當她還是小孩子時，就會游泳了。）
　　　　　　　 a kid.

（注意）請務必比較這兩句的時態。

<< 可能性 >>　1. The news of his death can't be　（關於他去世的消息不可能是真的。幾
　　　　　　　　 true. I just talked to him a few　 分鐘前我才剛和他說過話。）
　　　　　　　　 minutes ago.
　　　　　　 2. He said that it couldn't be　（他說那不可能是真的。）
　　　　　　　　 true.
　　　　　　 3. The news could be true.　　　（這消息也許是對的。）

（注意）could 表示可能性時，除了可用在過去式的句子中，也可用在現在式的句子中，但意義較 can 委婉。

<< 許可 >>　1. Can I open the window?　　　（我可以把窗子打開嗎？）
　　　　　　2. Could you keep silent?　　　（你可以保持安靜嗎？）

（注意）can 和 could 表示「許可」時，無時態之分；但 could 的用法較客氣、委婉。

can 與 could 可以用來表示「推測過去可能發生的事」，句型為：
(1) S + can/could have PP + ... ⇨推測過去可能發生的事
(2) S + can't/couldn't have PP + ... ⇨推測過去不可能發生的事

Examples:

　1. My brother could have done the housework.　（我弟弟可能把家事做好了。）
　2. Amy can't have been to a pub.　　　　　　（Amy 不可能到過酒吧。）

can 的另一個重要句型，是用來表達「不得不」：
S + cannot but + V= S + cannot help but+ V

Example:

It's raining outside. We <u>cannot but stay</u> at home. 　（外面在下雨，我們不得不待在家裡。）

= It's raining outside. We <u>cannot help but stay</u> at home.

Try This !

I. 填入適當的情態助動詞 can, can't, could, couldn't 使句意完整。

1. She used to have a good voice and ＿＿＿＿＿＿ sing very well. But she doesn't sing anymore after the operation.

2. Judy ＿＿＿＿＿＿ find her new belt. Has anyone seen it?

3. ＿＿＿＿＿＿ you show our new product to them? I have to answer an important phone call.

4. Ian ＿＿＿＿＿＿ have gone to Japan. He has to take the examination today!

5. My sister ＿＿＿＿＿＿ have cleaned my room for me. She is the laziest person in my family.

II. 根據中文完成英文句子。

1. 我們不得不戴口罩與量體溫。

We ＿＿＿＿＿＿ ＿＿＿＿＿＿ ＿＿＿＿＿＿ a mask and take temperature.

2. Kelly 不喜歡運動。她不可能去慢跑。

Kelly doesn't like exercise. She ＿＿＿＿＿＿ ＿＿＿＿＿＿ ＿＿＿＿＿＿ jogging.

四、would

would 一般用來表示過去習慣與請求。當表示「請求」時，比 will 的用法更客氣些。

Examples:

| << 過去習慣 >> | Jimmy would go jogging when he was young. | （當 Jimmy 年輕時，他都會慢跑。） |
| << 請求 >> | Would you turn on the light? | （可以請你開個燈嗎？） |

would 表達「提供、邀請或想要」的句型：
(1) 提供或邀請：Would/Wouldn't + S + like + N/to V...?
(2) 想要：S + would like to + V....

Examples:

<< 提供 >>	Would you like a piece of cake?	（要不要來塊蛋糕呢？）
<< 邀請 >>	Would you like to play volleyball?	（要不要一塊打排球呢？）
<< 想要 >>	Judy would like to buy me a present.	（Judy 想要買禮物給我。）

would 表達「寧願」以及「寧可…也不要」的句型：
(1) 寧願：S + would rather + 原形動詞
(2) 寧可…也不要：S + would rather + 原形動詞 + than + 原形動詞

Examples:

1. They would rather go to Hong Kong. （他們寧願到香港去。）
2. I would rather die than marry you! （我寧可死也不要嫁給你！）

五、may & might

may 與 might 都可以表達「請求許可」與「推測」，其中 may 是比較正式的用字，也比 can, could 都來得正式。

Examples:

| << 請求許可 >> | 1. May I go home now? | （我現在可以回家了嗎？） |
| | 2. You might not eat those strawberries. | （你不可以吃那些草莓。） |

<< 推測 >>　　1. He <u>may get</u> sick today.　　　　　　（他今天可能生病了。）
　　　　　　　2. She <u>might win</u> the game today.　　（她今天可能會贏得比賽。）

---

may 表達「祈願、祝福」的句型：May + S + V

Example:

　May <u>God</u> bless <u>you</u>!　　　　　　　　　　（願神保佑你！）

---

may 與 might 表達「…是理所當然的」、「最好」、「與其…不如…」等的句型：
(1) 有足夠的理由：S + may well + V
(2) 最好：S + may/might as well + V = S + had better + V
(3) 與其做 B 不如做 A：S + may/might as well A as B

Examples:

1. You study so hard. You <u>may well get</u> the scholarship.　　（你這麼用功，理當得到獎學金。）

2. It's getting late. You <u>might as well go</u> home.　　（天色漸晚，你最好回家去。）

3. You <u>may as well</u> throw your money away <u>as</u> lend it to John.　　（你與其把錢借給 John，不如把錢給丟了算了。）

Try This !

I. 填入適當的情態助動詞 would, may, might 使句意完整。

1. My brother ＿＿＿＿＿＿ play tennis when he was in the elementary school.

2. You ＿＿＿＿＿＿ leave as long as you tell me the truth.

3. Those students ＿＿＿＿＿＿ not leave the school unless the teacher let them go.

II. 根據中文完成英文句子。

1. 她寧願餓死，也不會拿他的錢。

　She ＿＿＿＿＿ ＿＿＿＿＿ starve to death ＿＿＿＿＿ take his money.

2. 媽媽辛苦工作了一整年，理當去度個假。

　Mother has been working hard for the whole year. She ＿＿＿＿＿ ＿＿＿＿＿ go on a vacation.

3. 你與其花錢買漫畫書，不如把錢捐給慈善機關。

　You ＿＿＿＿＿ ＿＿＿＿＿ ＿＿＿＿＿ donate your money to charities ＿＿＿＿＿ spend it on comic books.

六、must

must 是一個語氣十分強烈的情態助動詞，可以用來表達「強烈的勸戒或義務」、「強烈的禁止」與「肯定的推論」。

Examples:

<< 強烈勸戒 >>   Your father <u>must</u> stop smoking.
（你父親一定要戒菸。）

<< 義務 >>   I <u>must</u> finish my homework tonight.
（我必須今晚把功課做完。）

<< 強烈禁止 >>   You <u>mustn't</u> drive when you are drunk!
（你喝醉酒時，千萬不能開車！）

<< 肯定推論 >>   Mary is absent today. She <u>must</u> be sick.
（Mary 今天缺席，她一定是生病了。）

注意 — must, can, could, may, might 都可以用來表示「推測」，但可能性最高的是 must，could 最低。

must 用來表示對「過去」的「肯定推測」句型：
S + must + have + PP

Example:

The ground is wet this morning. It <u>must have</u> rained last night.   （今天早上地是濕的，昨晚一定下過雨。）

must 沒有過去式與未來式。但 must = have to，因此 **must** 的過去式與未來式都要藉助 have to 來表達。

Examples:

1. Rachel <u>had to</u> call me back last night, but she didn't.   （Rachel 昨晚必須回電給我，但她沒打。）

2. Tom <u>will have to</u> take his father to the hospital tomorrow.   （Tom 明天必須帶他父親去醫院。）

must 的答句
Must + S + V...?　Yes, S + must.（肯定）
　　　　　　　　　No, S + needn't.（否定）

Example:

1. A: Must I go now?　　　　　　　　　　　（A：我現在一定得去嗎？）
   B: Yes, you must.　　　　　　　　　　　（B：是的，現在就去。）
2. A: Must I finish all the food?　　　　　（A：我一定得吃完所有食物嗎?）
   B: No, you needn't.　　　　　　　　　　（B：不，你不需要。）

Try This !

I. 填入適當的情態助動詞 must, have to，並做適當的動詞變化，使句意完整。

1. You _____ (go) home right away. The whole family is waiting for you.
2. They will _____ (make) a decision if they want to sell their house before tomorrow.
3. Children _____ (not go) swimming alone. It is very dangerous.
4. Somebody _____ (have eaten) my cake. It's gone.
5. No matter what you see, you _____ (not tell) others about it.
6. They look sad. Their team _____ (have lost) the big game.

II. 根據中文完成英文句子。

1. 他們一定為他們走失的小狗感到擔心。
   They _____ _____ been worried about their lost dog.
2. 我們現在所要做的是好好計劃這場舞會。
   All we _____ _____ do now is to plan the party well.
3. 我一定要馬上開始工作嗎？不，你不需要。
   _____ I start working right now? No, you _____ .
4. 我明天必須參加一個重要的會議。
   I will _____ _____ attend an important meeting tomorrow.

I. 選出正確的答案。

1. _____ the story be true? He likes to tell jokes all the time.
   (A) Must (B) Can (C) Will (D) Should

2. You can't judge a person only by his looks. You _____ be wrong about him.
   (A) might (B) would (C) must (D) shall

3. Excuse me, _____ I look at the newest watch, please?
   (A) should (B) will (C) may (D) do

4. My little brother _____ hold his breath under water for 10 minutes.
   (A) must be (B) will have (C) would (D) can

5. When I was a child, my family _____ spend our summer vacation in Kenting.
   (A) would (B) should (C) might (D) could

6. Students _____ not cheat in exams, or they will be kicked out of the school.
   (A) must (B) would (C) have (D) might

7. Julia _____ have been sick. I saw her shopping in the department store yesterday.
   (A) wouldn't (B) must (C) couldn't (D) might

8. _____ you like some cherries or apples?
   (A) Might (B) Could (C) Will (D) Would

9. The doctor said that you _____ take some medicine and have more sleep.
   (A) should (B) may (C) could (D) will

10. Because they don't have a car, they _____ take a taxi to the restaurant.
    (A) had to (B) cannot but (C) cannot help (D) mustn't

11. John _____ me last night, but he didn't. I'm sure he forgot about this.
    (A) must have called (B) would call
    (C) called (D) should have called

12. We didn't visit our grandmother often. But when we _____, we stayed with her for hours.
    (A) do (B) could (C) had (D) did

13. Uncle Ken has been working hard on the farm through the whole year. He _____ take a vacation to reward himself.

(A) would rather　(B) had better　(C) may well　(D) may as well

14. They haven't tried the new flavor of Coke Cola, and _____ we.

(A) neither have　(B) so haven't　(C) neither do　(D) so don't

15. _____ we have a lot of rain this year.

(A) Will　(B) Shall　(C) Can　(D) May

II. 配合題。

_____ 16. Mary wears a wedding ring.

_____ 17. He is only twelve years old.

_____ 18. That lady holds a baby in her arms.

_____ 19. His eyes are red.

_____ 20. He drives a nice and expensive car.

(A) He can't be a college student.

(B) He could be a rich man.

(C) She may be the baby's mother.

(D) He might not sleep well last night.

(E) She must be married.

III. 挑錯並改正。

(   ) _____ 21. Kelly (A)would rather (B)buying a new car (C)than use a second-hand (D)one.

(   ) _____ 22. It's (A)boiling hot outside. We (B)can't help (C)but (D)rushing to the swimming pool.

(   ) _____ 23. You (A)can as well put me (B)to death (C)as ask me (D)to clean the toilet.

(   ) _____ 24. Mary (A)shall not (B)have been married (C)to her boyfriend (D)without telling her parents.

(   ) _____ 25. My father (A)got an emergency call two days (B)ago, and (C)must (D)fly to San Francisco right away.

(   ) _____ 26. "(A)Shall you (B)like to play cards with us?" "(C)I'd love to, but I (D)have to study for the test."

所謂的假設語氣就是表達「與事實不符」的語氣。在英文裡,要藉由「動詞時態的改變」來表達,區分為「與現在事實相反」、「與過去事實相反」及「與未來事實相反」三種。

假設語氣的基本句型:

If(如果;假如) + 條件子句,+ 主要子句 = 主要子句 + **if** + 條件子句

 5-1 與「現在事實相反」的假設語氣

與現在事實相反的假設語氣基本句型與說明如下:

基本句型:

$$\text{If} + \text{S} + \text{were/過去式動詞} , \text{S} + \begin{Bmatrix} \text{would/should} \\ \text{could/might} \end{Bmatrix} + \text{原形動詞}$$

說明:

(1) if 引導的條件子句使用過去式(be 動詞一律用 were)。

(2) 主要子句使用過去式助動詞 (would, should, could, might) + 原形動詞。

Examples:

1. If I <u>had</u> enough money, I <u>could buy</u> that red sports car.

(如果我有足夠的錢,我就可以買下那部紅色跑車了。)

2. If Tom Cruise <u>were</u> my husband, I <u>would be</u> the happiest woman in the world.

(如果湯姆克魯斯是我老公,我就會是全世界最快樂的女人了。)

3. If Anna <u>didn't have to</u> prepare for her final exam, she <u>might go</u> to the party.

(如果 Anna 不用準備期末考,她就可能會去舞會了。)

4. If I <u>were</u> free, I <u>should be</u> glad to travel with you.

(如果我有空,我會很樂意與你一同旅行。)

注意 — 表示與「現在事實」相反時,if 條件子句裡的<u>動詞用</u>「<u>過去式</u>」;但 be 動詞一律用 were。

I. 選出正確的答案。

☐ 1. If I _____ you, I _____ my best to help the poor girl.
    (A) am, will try   (B) was, would try
    (C) were, would try   (D) are, would to try

☐ 2. If Joan had free time, she _____ to the concert with you. Unfortunately, she has to finish her report today.
    (A) will have gone   (B) may go   (C) would have gone (D) might go

☐ 3. There is something wrong with the computer. It _____ well as usual if you didn't get someone to fix it.
    (A) couldn't work   (B) can't work   (C) couldn't worked (D) won't work

☐ 4. I _____ call her right now if I _____ her phone number.
    (A) will, had   (B) would, had   (C) would have, had (D) must, had

II. 根據提供的事實，填入適當的動詞，以完成下列的假設句。

1. 事實：Mary isn't here today.
   If Mary (*be*) _____ here today, she _____ (*help*) you finish this job.

2. 事實：My mother doesn't read the newspaper.
   If my mother (*read*) _____ the newspaper, she _____ (*learn about*) the big sales in SOGO.

III. 根據中文完成英文句子。

1. 如果媽媽看到你現在還在打電動，她一定會抓狂。
   Mother _____ go mad _____ she _____ you still playing computer games now.

2. 如果我今天沒那麼疲倦，我就可以和妳一起去看電影。
   If I _____ not so tired today, I _____ _____ to the movies with you.

5-2 與「過去事實相反」的假設語氣

與過去事實相反的假設語氣基本句型與說明如下：

基本句型：

$$\text{If} + \text{S} + \text{had} + \text{PP}，\text{S} + \begin{Bmatrix} \text{would/should} \\ \text{could/might} \end{Bmatrix} + \text{have} + \text{PP}$$

說明：

(1) if 引導的條件子句使用過去完成式 (had + PP)。

(2) 主要子句用過去式助動詞 (would, should, could, might) + 現在完成式 (have PP)。

Examples:

1. If Joe <u>had known</u> of your arrival, he <u>might have met</u> you at the airport.

（如果 Joe 知道你來，他就會去機場與你見面。）

2. If John <u>had worn</u> enough clothes yesterday, he <u>would</u> not <u>have caught</u> a cold.

（如果 John 昨天衣服穿夠的話，他就不會感冒了。）

注意 ➡ 表示與「過去事實」相反時，if 條件子句裡的動詞用「過去完成式」。

有時候，一句話中可能會同時出現「條件子句與過去事實相反」，但是「主要子句與現在事實相反」，此時：

(1) 條件子句使用過去完成式。

(2) 主要子句使用過去式助動詞 (would, should, could, might) + 原形動詞。

Examples:

1. If I <u>had studied</u> harder yesterday, I <u>wouldn't fail</u> the math test now.

（如果我昨天用功一點，現在數學考試就不會不及格了。）

2. If Stanley <u>had not been</u> late this morning, he <u>would not be punished</u> by the Dean of the Students' Affairs now.

（如果 Stanley 今天早上沒有遲到，現在就不會被訓導主任處罰了。）

Try This!

I. 選出正確的答案。

☐ 1. If Miss Yen _____ in the classroom yesterday morning, she _____ what had happened.
    (A) were, would know   (B) had been, would have known
    (C) is, will know   (D) were, would have known

☐ 2. Amy _____ the beautiful dress last week if she _____ enough money with her.
    (A) bought, had   (B) would buy, had had
    (C) might have bought, had had   (D) will, has

☐ 3. If I _____ harder last year, I _____ more money now.
    (A) had worked, would have   (B) worked, would have
    (C) have been working, will have (D) had worked, would have had

☐ 4. Tom _____ a successful businessman now if he had not been so lazy before.
    (A) might be   (B) may be   (C) might have been (D) will be

II. 根據提供的事實，填入適當的動詞，以完成下列的假設句。

1. 事實：He didn't find any job last year. He couldn't give the money back to you.
If he _____ (*find*) a job last year, he _____ (*give*) the money back to you.

2. 事實：It didn't rain last month. We don't have enough water now.
If it _____ (*rain*) a lot last month, we _____ (*have*) enough water now.

III. 根據中文完成英文句子。

1. 如果 Johnson 昨天在這裡的話，他不會讓這件事情發生的。
If Johnson _____ _____ here yesterday, he would not _____ _____ this happen.

2. 如果昨天晚上沒有下雨，現在地上就不會溼了。
The ground _____ not _____ wet if it _____ not _____ last night.

3. 要是當時我盡全力用功讀書的話，我現在可能已經是個清大的學生了。
If I _____ tried my best to study, I _____ be a student of National Tsing Hua University now.

5–3　與「未來事實相反」的假設語氣

與未來事實相反的假設語氣 (1) 表示「不可能發生」的假設語氣用：were to
基本句型：

$$\text{If} + S_1 + \text{were to} + V_1, S_2 + \begin{Bmatrix} \text{would/should} \\ \text{could/might} \end{Bmatrix} + \text{原形 } V_2$$

Examples:

1. If the sun <u>were to rise</u> in the west tomorrow morning, I <u>would marry</u> you.
   （如果明天太陽從西邊出來，我就嫁給你。）

2. If the oceans <u>were to dry</u>, human beings <u>would</u> surely <u>die out</u>.
   （要是海洋都乾掉了，人類就一定會滅亡。）

與未來事實相反的假設語氣 (2) 表示「萬一」的假設語氣用：should
基本句型：

$$\text{If} + S_1 + \text{should} + V_1, S_2 + \begin{Bmatrix} \text{would/should/could/might} \\ \text{或 will/shall/can/may} \end{Bmatrix} + \text{原形 } V_2$$

Examples:

1. If your son <u>should get</u> sick tomorrow, what <u>would</u> you <u>do</u>?
   （萬一你的兒子明天生病的話，你會怎麼辦？）

2. If you <u>should fall</u> into this lake, you <u>will be</u> drowned.
   （萬一你掉到這個湖裡，你鐵定會淹死。）

5–4　假設語氣中 **if** 的省略

If 為首的條件子句，如有出現 were, had, should 時，可以把它們移到句首，並去掉 if。
句型： $\begin{Bmatrix} \text{Were} + S + \text{N/Adj} \\ \text{Had} + S + \text{PP} \\ \text{Should} + S + \text{原形動詞} \end{Bmatrix}, S + \begin{Bmatrix} \text{would/should} \\ \text{could/might} \end{Bmatrix} + \begin{Bmatrix} \text{原形動詞} \\ \text{have} + \text{PP} \end{Bmatrix}$

Examples:

1. If I <u>were</u> a girl, I would fall in love with Jacky Chen.

   = <u>Were</u> I a girl, I would fall in love with Jacky Chen.

   （如果我是女生，我會愛上成龍。）

2. If he <u>had</u> had enough time, he would have solved this problem.

   = <u>Had</u> he had enough time, he would have solved this problem.

   （如果他的時間足夠，他就會解決這個問題。）

3. What would you do if you <u>should</u> face the president?

   = What would you do <u>should</u> you face the president?

   （萬一你面對總統，你會怎麼辦？）

I. 選出正確的答案。

☐ 1. If the sun _____, there would be no living things in this world.

(A) disappear　　　　　　(B) would disappear

(C) were to disappear　　　(D) had disappeared

☐ 2. _____ my mom give me 1,000 dollars tomorrow, I could buy the game I've wanted for so long.

(A) If　　　　(B) Should　　　　(C) Were　　　　(D) Had

☐ 3. If the air crash _____ happen during your vacation, what can I do?

(A) were　　　　(B) had　　　　(C) should　　　　(D) might

II. 根據中文完成英文句子。

1. 如果我去年有錢的話，我就可以買下這棟房子。

   _____ I had money last year, I could _____ bought the house.

2. 如果我可以重生的話，我要成為一個畫家。

   If I _____ _____ be reborn, I would become a painter.

3. 萬一你開車時打起瞌睡，很容易發生車禍。

   If you _____ doze off when driving, a car crash _____ happen easily.

5–5　wish 的用法

wish 的意義為「但願」，表達的是「不可能實現的願望」，因此它之後通常是接假設語氣的子句：

(1) 願望是與現在事實相反時，其後子句的動詞用「過去式」，若是 be 動詞一律用 were：

　　S + wish (+ that) + S + were/過去式動詞

(2) 願望是與過去事實相反時，其後子句的動詞用「過去完成式 (had + PP)」：

　　S +wish(ed) (+ that) + S + had PP

Examples:

1. I wish (that) I were a bird.　　　　　　　　　　　　　（但願我是一隻鳥。）

　　⇨事實上，我不是一隻鳥，所以 be 動詞用 were。

2. We wish (that) we didn't have any test today.　　　（我們希望今天沒有任何

　　⇨事實上，我們今天有考試，所以動詞用 didn't have。　考試。）

3. Linda wished (that) she had not been sick the week　（Linda 希望她上個禮拜
　　before.　　　　　　　　　　　　　　　　　　　　沒有生病。）

　　⇨事實上，Linda 上個禮拜生病了，所以動詞用 had not been。

注意　一般很有可能實現的願望，我們用 hope，不會用 wish。

I wish + that 子句的句子，幾乎都可以用 If only....（但願…。）來代換，用法與 wish 相同。

Examples:

1. If only I could fly.

　　⇨ I wish that I could fly.

　　（但願我能飛。）

2. If only I had passed the exam yesterday.

　　⇨ I wish that I had passed the exam yesterday.

　　（但願我昨天有通過考試。）

5-6　as if 與 as though

另外經常和假設語氣連用的片語有 as if 或 as though（彷彿，好像）。

句型為：S + V + as if/as though + 假設句

Examples:

1. He talks <u>as if</u> he <u>knew</u> everything.

   （他講得好像他什麼都知道。）⇨事實是「他什麼都不知道」。

2. The man behaved <u>as though</u> nothing <u>had happened</u>.

   （這個男人表現得好像什麼都沒發生過。）⇨事實是「有事情發生了」。

I. 選出正確的答案。

☐ 1. I wish that I _____ to Italy this summer vacation.

   (A) could go　　(B) can go　　(C) have to go　　(D) will go

☐ 2. Helen really wished that you _____ her the truth.

   (A) had had told　　(B) tell　　(C) telling　　(D) had told

☐ 3. _____ I didn't have to go to school.

   (A) I wished　　(B) If only　　(C) As if　　(D) Wishing

☐ 4. He looks as if _____.

   (A) he knew nothing about it

   (B) he hadn't known anything about it

   (C) he is knowing nothing about it

   (D) he had known anything about it

II. 根據中文完成英文句子。

1. Julia 希望住在一間很大的房子裡。

   Julia wishes that she _____ in a large house.

2. 但願我再年輕一點就好了！

   If only I _____ a little younger!

I. 選出正確的答案。

1. What will you buy _____ you have one million dollars in hand?
   (A) had   (B) were   (C) should   (D) was

2. Lee wished that he _____ such a stupid thing in front of the girl he liked.
   (A) didn't do   (B) wouldn't do   (C) hadn't done   (D) doesn't do

3. _____ I practiced enough, I might have won the first prize in the speech contest.
   (A) If   (B) When   (C) Had   (D) Have

4. The students wish that they _____ any test and exam at school.
   (A) didn't have   (B) don't have   (C) won't have   (D) are not having

5. If Max _____ his leg, he would have joined us in the basketball game.
   (A) had not hurt   (B) didn't hurt
   (C) was not hurt   (D) isn't hurt

6. If Dr. Sun Yat-sen _____ here tomorrow, I would give you one million dollars.
   (A) had come   (B) should come   (C) were to come   (D) would come

7. If James _____ the general manager, he would _____ the lazy bone right now.
   (A) is, fire   (B) was, have fired
   (C) were, fire   (D) were, have fired

8. If Violet _____ the truth to her teacher yesterday, she _____ so guilty now.
   (A) told, won't feel   (B) had told, wouldn't feel
   (C) had told, hadn't felt   (D) told, won't feel

II. 根據中文完成英文句子。

9. 如果我們沒有那麼多考試，我們可能會更快樂。

   If we _____ _____ so many tests, we _____ _____ happier.

10. 如果 Ben 當時有聽父母的話，他就不會跟同學打架了。

    If Ben _____ _____ to his parents, he wouldn't have _____ with his classmates.

11. 如果早上火車不誤點，我就會準時上班。

    If the train _____ delayed this morning, I would _____ _____ in the office on time.

12. 萬一下禮拜二我中樂透頭獎的話，我就捐五百萬給那家孤兒院。

    If I _____ win the first prize in the Lottery next Tuesday, I _____ donate 5 million dollars to that orphanage.

    (= _____ I win the first prize in the Lottery next Tuesday, I _____ donate 5 million dollars to that orphanage.)

13. 如果沒有陽光、空氣和水，世界上就沒有生物了。

    It there _____ no sunshine, air, and water, there _____ _____ no living things in the world.

14. 要是你曾經看過鐵達尼號，你現在就會知道 Rose 要的愛情是什麼了。

    If you _____ _____ the movie "Titanic," you _____ _____ the love Rose wants.

III. 選擇框中適當的子句完成下列句子。

(A) nobody will know it
(B) if Gandalf had been there with him
(C) if those drivers had really obeyed the traffic rules
(D) you wouldn't be so rude and impolite now
(E) I wished he had not seen me

15. Frodo would not be so sad _____.
16. If you don't tell the truth, _____.
17. If you had been well-educated when you were a child, _____.
18. The boy I feared most was right there; _____.
19. There would not have been so many deaths and injuries _____.

在英文裡，有時候我們無法用一個簡單的形容詞來描述一個名詞；這時，就需要用「關係代名詞」放在名詞之後，引導一個形容詞子句來作修飾。所謂「關係代名詞」，又簡稱「關代」，是兼具「代名詞」與「連接詞」雙重作用的詞類；在不同的情況下，會使用不同性質的關代；其後所引導的形容詞子句，就是「關係子句」，是用來修飾前面的「先行詞」。所謂「先行詞」，則是指關係代名詞所代替的「名詞」，通常就是關係代名詞前面所出現的名詞。

關係代名詞的種類

格 先行詞	主格	受格	所有格
人	who	whom	whose
事物或動物	which	which	whose
人 + 事物或動物	that	that	

6–1　先行詞為「人」的關係代名詞與關係子句

先行詞為「人」，關係代名詞在子句中作主格時，關代用 who。

Examples:

1. That woman is Julia Roberts. That woman has a big mouth.

   ⇒ That woman who has a big mouth is Julia Roberts.

   （那個有大嘴巴的女人是 Julia Roberts。）⇒劃線部份用來形容前面先行詞 "The woman"

2. Do you know the boy? The boy came here this morning.

   ⇒ Do you know the boy who came here this morning?

   （你認識今天早上來過這裡的男孩嗎？）

先行詞為「人」，關係代名詞在子句中作受格時，

(1) 關代用 whom；

(2) 受格的關代有時是動詞或介系詞的受詞，形成關係子句時可以：

　　(a) 介系詞若是片語動詞的一部分，得保留在動詞後面，

　　(b) 介系詞若非片語動詞的一部分，可移到關代的前面或放在動詞後面。

Examples:

1. The girl enjoys swimming very much. I met <u>the girl</u> at the party yesterday.

   ⇨ The girl <u>whom I met at the party yesterday</u> enjoys swimming very much.

   （那位<u>我昨天在舞會上遇見的</u>女孩很喜歡游泳。）⇨劃線部份用來形容前面的先行詞 "The girl"。

2. Is this <u>the lady</u> <u>whom you spoke of?</u> （這就是<u>你提過的</u>那位小姐嗎？）

3. He is the man <u>whom I have immense respect for.</u>

   = He is the man <u>for whom I have immense respect.</u>

   他是<u>我非常尊敬的</u>一位男士。

先行詞為「人」，關係代名詞在子句中作所有格時，關代用 whose。

Examples:

1. I know <u>that boy.</u> <u>That boy's</u> father is a PE teacher.

   ⇨ I know that boy <u>whose father is a PE teacher.</u>

   （我認識<u>那位父親是體育老師的</u>男孩。）⇨劃線部份用來形容前面的先行詞 "the boy"

2. <u>The old lady</u> likes to go jogging. <u>Her</u> sports shoes are red.

   ⇨ The old lady <u>whose sports shoes are red</u> likes jogging.

   （那位<u>運動鞋是紅色的</u>老太太喜歡慢跑。）

Try This !

I. 填入適當的關係代名詞，以完成句子。

1. The student _____ is playing the guitar is Helen.

2. Do you know the woman _____ we met at the party yesterday?

3. I don't know the boy _____ is playing volleyball.

II. 用適當的關係代名詞合併句子。

1. That boy likes to play golf. That boy is sitting under the tree.

   ⇨_____

2. The beautiful girl is Pinky. The beautiful girl's eyes are blue.

   ⇨_____

6-2　先行詞為「事物或動物」的關係代名詞與關係子句

先行詞為「事物或動物」，關係代名詞在子句中作主格時，關代用 which。

Examples:

1. That pen is mine. That pen is on the desk.　（那枝在桌上的筆是我的。）
   ⇨ That pen which is on the desk is mine.　⇨劃線部份用來形容前面的 "The pen"。
2. I like that dog. That dog has golden hair.　（我喜歡那隻有金黃色毛的狗。）
   ⇨ I like that dog which has golden hair.

先行詞為「事物或動物」，關係代名詞在子句中作受格時，
(1) 關代為 which。
(2) 受格的關代有時是動詞或介系詞的受詞，形成關係子句時可以：
　　(a) 介系詞若是片語動詞的一部分，得保留在動詞後面，
　　(b) 介系詞若非片語動詞的一部分，可移到關代的前面或放在動詞後面。

Examples:

1. Please fetch the book for me. I bought the book yesterday.
   ⇨ Please fetch the book which I bought yesterday for me.
   （請替我把我昨天買的書拿來。）⇨劃線部份用來形容前面的 "the book"。
2. The picture was painted by my brother. You are looking at the picture.
   ⇨ The picture which you are looking at was painted by my brother.
   （你們現在所看到的這幅畫是我弟弟所畫的。）
3. That is the house which they live in.
   = That is the house in which they live.
   （那是他們居住的房子。）

先行詞為「事物或動物」，關係代名詞為所有格時，關代用 whose。

Examples:

1. Suzanne likes that doll. That doll's dress is pink.

⇨ Suzanne likes that doll whose dress is pink.

（Suzanne 很喜歡那個穿粉紅色洋裝的洋娃娃。）⇨劃線部份用來形容前面的 "the doll"

2. That cute dog is Joan's pet. That cute dog's eyes are big and round.

⇨ That cute dog whose eyes are big and round is Joan's pet.

（那隻眼睛又大又圓的可愛狗狗是 Joan 的寵物。）

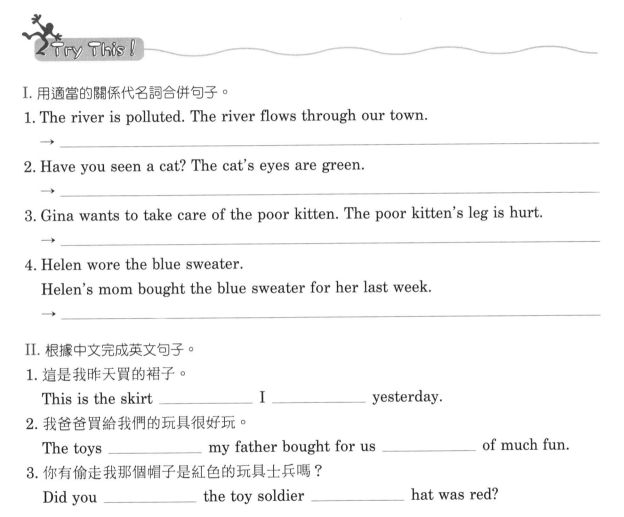

Try This !

I. 用適當的關係代名詞合併句子。

1. The river is polluted. The river flows through our town.

→ _____

2. Have you seen a cat? The cat's eyes are green.

→ _____

3. Gina wants to take care of the poor kitten. The poor kitten's leg is hurt.

→ _____

4. Helen wore the blue sweater.

Helen's mom bought the blue sweater for her last week.

→ _____

II. 根據中文完成英文句子。

1. 這是我昨天買的裙子。

This is the skirt _____ I _____ yesterday.

2. 我爸爸買給我們的玩具很好玩。

The toys _____ my father bought for us _____ of much fun.

3. 你有偷走我那個帽子是紅色的玩具士兵嗎？

Did you _____ the toy soldier _____ hat was red?

6-3 先行詞為「人 + 事物或動物」的關係子句

先行詞為「人 + 事物或動物」，

(1) 無論作主格、受格，關係代名詞都用 that；

(2) 沒有關係代名詞為所有格的情況。

Examples:

《主格》 The little girl and her cat are both cute. They are in the garden.

→ The little girl and her cat that are in the garden are both cute.

（在花園裡的小女孩與她的貓都很可愛。）

《受格》 The kid and his pet dog were scared to death. The bad man kidnapped them.

→ The kid and his pet dog that the bad man kidnapped were scared to death.

（遭壞人綁架的小孩與他的小狗都被嚇壞了。）

用適當的關係代名詞合併句子。

1. The woman and her cat look very peaceful.

The woman and her cat are sitting on the bench.

→ _____

2. The woman and her car are still fine.

The truck hit the woman and her car.

→ _____

3. The man and the statue look like twin brothers.

The man and the statue are standing side by side.

→ _____

4. The beauty and the snake are giving a performance together in the square.

We saw the beauty and the snake at the market last week.

→ _____

6-4　關係代名詞的限定用法與非限定（補述）用法

限定與非限定的差別：

限定用法	非限定（補述）用法
當關係代名詞前沒有加逗點 " , " 時，其所引導的形容詞子句，是用來限定先行詞的。	當關係代名詞前有加逗點 " , " 時，其所引導的形容詞子句，是用來補充說明先行詞。

Examples:

限定用法	非限定（補述）用法
1. My sister who is in Taipei will come here tomorrow. （我在臺北的姊姊明天要來這裡。） →「不只」一位姊姊，而其中一位在臺北。	1. My sister, who is in Taipei, will come here tomorrow. （我姊姊，人在臺北，明天會來這裡。） →「只有」一位姊姊，而且人在臺北。
2. His uncle who likes to drink had a car accident yesterday. （他那喜歡喝酒的叔叔昨天出車禍。） →「不只」一位叔叔，而其中這位頗愛喝酒。	2. His uncle, who likes to drink, had a car accident yesterday. （他叔叔，喜歡喝酒，昨天出車禍。） →「只有」一位叔叔，而且頗愛喝酒。
3. Their cat which has brown eyes likes to catch mice. （他們那隻有棕色眼睛的貓咪喜歡抓老鼠。） →「不只」一隻貓咪，而其中這隻有棕色眼睛。	3. Their cat, which has brown eyes, likes to catch mice. （他們那隻貓，眼睛棕色，喜歡抓老鼠。） →「只有」一隻貓，而且牠的眼睛是棕色的。

注意 ★ 請務必比較左右兩句之間的差異性！

描述某個特定的人、事、物或專有名詞，務必使用「非限定（補述）用法」。

Examples:

1. My father, who was a soldier before, is a man with a strong sense of responsibility.

（我的父親，以前是軍人，是個有強烈責任感的男人。）

2. Mel Gibson, whose eyes are green, is a famous movie star.

(Mel Gibson，他的眼睛是綠色的，是個很有名的電影明星。)

3. Big Ben, which we visited last summer, is one of the famous spots in England.

(大笨鐘，我們去年夏天參觀過，是英國有名的景點之一。)

4. I like Vincent van Gogh, whose paintings are full of passion.

(我喜歡梵谷，他的畫充滿激情。)

I. 用適當的關係代名詞合併句子。

1. My mom takes good care of us. My mom is a tender woman.

→ _____

2. Mr. Lin is a very serious teacher. Mr. Lin teaches us Chinese.

→ _____

3. The *Mona Lisa* is a beautiful masterpiece. The *Mona Lisa* was created by Leonardo da Vinci.

→ _____

II. 填入適當的關係代名詞使句意完整。

1. The Great Wall, _____ is the longest construction in the world, is world-famous.

2. My brother, _____ my grandpa loves most, moved to the big city two years ago.

3. Last Monday he went to Keelung, _____ is famous for its port.

4. "The Waste Land", _____ should be the most difficult poem in the 20th century, is written by T.S. Eliot.

5. Are you the man _____ I met on the top of the mountain last week?

6. That is the grave in _____ my mother is buried.

6-5   **that** 當關係代名詞的用法

that「可」替代限定用法中的關代 who、whom、which；
但「不可」替代非限定用法中的關代，也「不可」替代 whose。

Examples:

1. This is the watch <u>which</u> I like most.
   = This is the watch <u>that</u> I like most
   （這是我最喜歡的手錶。）

2. The girl <u>whom</u> you just mentioned is my best friend.
   = The girl <u>that</u> you just mentioned is my best friend.
   （你剛剛提到的女孩子是我最好的朋友。）

先行詞為「人 + 事物或動物」時，關代用 that。

Example:

Look at <u>the man and his dog</u> <u>that are crossing the bridge</u>.
（看看正在過橋的男人和他的狗。）

先行詞有：
(1) 「序數」（即「第一」、「第二」等的形容詞）；
(2) 「最高級」時，關代一律用 that。

Examples:

1. <u>The first student</u> <u>that came to school this morning</u> is Anna.
   （今天早上<u>第一</u>個到校的<u>學生</u>是 Anna。）

2. You are <u>the most beautiful girl</u> <u>that I have ever seen</u>.
   （妳是我所見過<u>最美麗</u>的女孩。）

先行詞含有下列單字或片語時，關代一律用 that：

the only（唯一的），any（任何），the same（相同的）

the very（正是）， all（全部）， no（無一），anyone（任何人）

Examples:

1. Hualien is the only place that I want to go for a visit.

（花蓮是我唯一想要去參觀的地方。）

2. Anyone that had believed in him was cheated.

（任何曾經相信他的人都被騙了。）

3. This is the same shampoo that I use every day.

（這是與我每天所用的一樣的洗髮精。）

4. You are the very man that I want to employ.

（你正是我想要雇用的人。）

5. This is all that I know about him.

（這是我所瞭解他的全部。）

6. There was no one that I knew.

（沒有一個我所認識的人。）

主要子句是 Who、Which、What 等疑問詞起首時，為避免誤會與重複，關代一律用 that。

Examples:

1. Who is the movie star that you want to see most?

（你最想看到的電影明星是哪一位？）

2. Which is the book that you borrowed from Annie?

（哪一本書是你跟 Annie 借的？）

在下面情況中不能使用 that：

(1) 關係代名詞為 whose，不能替換為 that。

(2) 關係子句是非限定補述用法時，關代不能用 that。

(3) 關代是受格，前面又加上介系詞（如 of which, in which 等），不能替換成 that。

　　（也就是說，不能出現 of that 這種寫法，除非把介系詞挪回子句動詞後。）

Example：（關於第三點的例子）

(○) This is the house in which he lives.

(○) This is the house that he lives in.

(×) This is the house in that he lives.

Try This!

I. 判斷下面句子裡的關係代名詞正確與否，對的請打○，錯的請打×，並改成正確的關代。

( ) _____ 1. You can ask any question which is about pop music.

( ) _____ 2. This is the very cat that stole my fish yesterday.

( ) _____ 3. This is the man about that we talked yesterday.

( ) _____ 4. The handsome boy that hair is blond is the leader of our school's soccer team.

( ) _____ 5. All the books that are given by Tommy are new and expensive.

( ) _____ 6. Beethoven, that music is still widely performed, is one of the greatest composers in the world.

( ) _____ 7. God helps those who help themselves.

II. 用適當的關係代名詞合併句子。

1. Who is the boy? The boy plays computer games over there.

　→ _____

2. Helen is the very person. I want to choose Helen as the class leader.

　→ _____

6-6　關係副詞 where, when

當關代引導的動詞片語裡有介系詞時，介系詞不可省略，但可以用關係副詞來取代。
關係副詞 = 介系詞 + 關係代名詞，使用什麼關係副詞，要看先行詞來決定。
(1) 先行詞為「地方」：關係副詞用 where。
(2) 先行詞為「時間」：關係副詞用 when。

Examples:

先行詞為「地方」

1. This is the house which he lives in.
   = This is the house in which he lives.
   = This is the house where he lives.
   （這就是他所住的房子。）　　⇨ where = in which

2. That is the river in which I went swimming in my childhood.
   =That is the river where I went swimming in my childhood.
   （這是我小時候游泳的河流。）　　⇨ where = in which

先行詞為「時間」

1. The Lantern Festival in 1973 was the day which I was born on.
   = The Lantern Festival in 1973 was the day on which I was born.
   = The Lantern Festival in 1973 was the day when I was born.
   （1973 年的元宵節是我出生的日子。）　　⇨ when = on which

2. Sunday is the day on which we go to church.
   = Sunday is the day when we go to church.
   （週日是我們上教堂的日子。）　　⇨ when = on which

關係副詞的先行詞若為 time、place，則可以省略。

Examples:

1. That was when (= the time when) I was still learning to walk.
   （那是我還在學走路的時候。）

2. The road leads us to where (= the place where) success lies.
   （這條道路引導我們到成功所在的地方。）

Try This !

填入適當的關係副詞，以完成句子。

1. Taipei is the city _____ I was born.

2. This forest is _____ you can catch a tiger alive.

3. June is the month _____ many students graduate from school.

4. The park near my house is _____ we used to play basketball.

5. The year 1929 is the year _____ the economy in the States fell down.

6-7 關係代名詞的省略及特殊用法

> 關代的直接省略：
> (1) 限定用法中，關代為受格 (whom, which, that) 時，可以省略。
> (2) 非限定用法中的受格關代 whom, which 不可以省略！
> (3) 關代為所有格 (whose) 時不可以省略！

Examples:

1. Isn't that the girl whom you are waiting for?
   = Isn't that the girl you are waiting for?
   （那不是你正在等待的女孩嗎？）
   ⇨限定用法，關代為受格 whom，可以省略。

2. (○) Domingo, whom we all love, is the best singer of the world.
   (×) Domingo, we all love, is the best singer of the world.
   （Domingo 是世界上最好的歌手，我們都喜愛他。）
   ⇨非限定用法中的關代為受格 whom 時，不可以省略。

> 特殊用法：
> (1) 當句子裡有「關代 + be V-ing/PP」時，通常可將「關代 + be」一起省略。
> (2) 當句子裡有「關代 + 一般動詞」時，可改寫為 V-ing 的形式，並去掉關代。

Examples:

1. The girl who is playing the guitar is Sheri.
   = The girl playing the guitar is Sheri.
   （在彈吉他的女孩是 Sheri。）
   ⇨關代 who + is 可一起省略。

2. The man who was chosen to be chairman bowed his thanks.
   = The man chosen to be chairman bowed his thanks.
   （被選為主席的男子鞠躬致謝。）

3. The man who sits in front of you is our boss.

= The man <u>sitting</u> in front of you is our boss.

（坐在你前面的是我們的老闆。）

⇨ 關代 who + 一般動詞 sit，可改寫為 sitting。

注意 想進一步探討重點 (2)，可參考第七章分詞構句。

請將以下各句的關係代名詞省略，並將整句進行必要的改寫。

1. The cake which we bought yesterday is very delicious.

　→ _____

2. This is the man who gave us this book.

　→ _____

3. The cat which always chases a mouse is now taking a sun bath.

　→ _____

4. The lady who is reading the novel in the café is my aunt.

　→ _____

✔Test & Review

I. 選出正確的答案。

☐ 1. I like the girl _____ hair is short and curly.
    (A) which   (B) whose   (C) that   (D) whom

☐ 2. The woman _____ riding a motorcycle is my friend.
    (A) who   (B) ×   (C) whom   (D) which

☐ 3. Where is the little cat _____ we saw under the tree just now?
    (A) who   (B) whose   (C) whom   (D) that

☐ 4. People _____ have high EQ usually take a more positive attitude toward everything.
    (A) who   (B) which   (C) whom   (D) what

☐ 5. Jane is the very woman _____ I want to marry.
    (A) which   (B) that   (C) what   (D) whose

☐ 6. Thanksgiving is the day _____ people show their gratitude to those _____ have helped them.
    (A) which, who   (B) when, whom   (C) when, who   (D) where, who

☐ 7. Here come the boy and his dog _____ we saw in the school yesterday.
    (A) that   (B) who   (C) whom   (D) which

☐ 8. Jacky Wu is the most humorous star _____ I have ever known.
    (A) who   (B) whom   (C) that   (D) which

☐ 9. Hsin-chu is the place _____ my boyfriend and I met for the first time.
    (A) which   (B) where   (C) when   (D) that

☐ 10. The person _____ in front of the house owns a big company.
    (A) who standing   (B) is standing   (C) standing   (D) stands

II. 根據中文完成英文句子。

11. 他穿的鞋子是新的。 The _____ he is wearing _____ new.

12. 我昨天遇見的女孩很有禮貌。

    _____ _____ _____ I met yesterday was polite.

13. Andy 是個很受歡迎的男生，他的眼睛小小的。

Andy, _____ eyes _____ small, _____ a very popular boy.

14. 不運動的人不健康。

_____ _____ don't take exercise _____ unhealthy.

15. 我那個已經寫了一早上的信的妹妹還只是個國中生。

My sister _____ _____ _____ writing letters all the morning is only a junior high school student.

III. 選擇框中適當選項以完成下列句子。

16. Which is the magazine _____?

17. New York is the place _____.

18. This is the same skirt _____.

19. The Eiffel Tower, _____, is a famous tourist spot in Paris.

(A) that I wore to Tina's party last week

(B) that you want to read first

(C) which is 320 meters high

(D) where many artists love to stay

IV. 將下列中文句子翻譯成英文。

20. Mr. Lee 是昨天最先離開辦公室的人。

_____

21. Flora 是我唯一信任的朋友。

_____

22. 在大城市生活的人通常不是很友善。

_____

7-1　　不定詞與動名詞—概說

(1) 不定詞與動名詞都是動詞的演變，雖然有動詞的樣子，但都已經不再是動詞，而是名詞，有時也兼具形容詞或副詞的性質。
(2) 基本的出現位置：當主詞、受詞與補語。
(3) 不定詞與動名詞作為名詞，都是單數名詞（因為都只代表一件事情）。

Examples:

<<當主詞>> 1. To make a right decision at the right time is not easy.
　　　　　　　　　　　　　　　　　S

（在正確的時刻做下正確的決定並不容易。）

2. Learning English well takes a lot of time.
　　　　　S

（把英語學好要花很多時間。）

<<當受詞>> 1. I try to make him understand what I am saying.
　　　　　　　　　　　　　　O

（我試著去讓他瞭解我到底在說什麼。）

2. Peter enjoys listening to music.
　　　　　　　　　O

（Peter 很喜歡聽音樂。）

<<當補語>> 1. Gina asked Wendy to give her a ride.
　　　　　　　　　　　　　　OC

（Gina 要 Wendy 載她一程。）

2. What I am afraid most at school is attending Mr. Kennedy's class.
　　　　　　　　　　　　　　　　　　　　　　　SC

（我在學校最怕的事是上 Mr. Kennedy 的課。）

一、後面常接不定詞的動詞

(1) 常接不定詞作受詞或受詞補語的常見動詞有：
　　want, need, hope, plan, decide, seem, offer, refuse,
　　care, promise, agree, expect, pretend, mean
(2) 不定詞的否定：S + V + not + to V

Examples:

    1. Lisa <u>decided</u> <u>to take</u> a plane to Kaohsiung. （Lisa 決定要搭機飛到高雄。）

    2. John <u>promised</u> me <u>not to smoke</u> anymore. （John 答應我不再抽菸了。）

二、後面只接動名詞的動詞

(1) 常見只接動名詞作受詞的動詞與片語動詞：
    enjoy, finish, quit, mind, keep, practice, deny, suggest,
    avoid, consider, imagine, miss, postpone, resist, discuss,
    think about, talk about, put off, keep on
(2) 動名詞的否定：$S + V_1 + not + V_2\text{-ing}$

Examples:

    1. My father has <u>quit</u> <u>drinking</u>. （我的父親已經戒酒了。）

    2. They <u>discussed</u> <u>not eating</u> meat anymore. （他們討論以後不再吃肉了。）

I. 請將括弧裡的動詞作適當變化，以完成句子。

1. Do you mind ＿＿＿＿＿＿ (*turn*) your radio down a little bit?

2. Joseph is keeping on ＿＿＿＿＿＿ (*play*) computer games.

3. Murray expects ＿＿＿＿＿＿ (*sing*) on the stage in the future.

4. Victoria has never considered ＿＿＿＿＿＿ (*marry*) a foreigner.

5. Nicklause hopes ＿＿＿＿＿＿ (*win*) the next golf tournament.

II. 根據中文完成英文句子。

1. 她希望有一天能成為有錢且能幹的職業婦女。

    She ＿＿＿＿＿ ＿＿＿＿＿ ＿＿＿＿＿ a rich and capable career woman someday.

2. Willy 承認他偷了一臺腳踏車，還把車子賣給別人。

    Willy admitted ＿＿＿＿＿＿ a bike and ＿＿＿＿＿＿ it to someone else.

3. 他不是有意傷害你的，忘記他所說的吧。

    He didn't mean ＿＿＿＿＿ ＿＿＿＿＿ you. Forget about what he said.

三、後面可接不定詞或動名詞但意義不同的動詞

某些動詞（如 like、intend）後面可以接動名詞，也可以接不定詞，且意義相同。
但是，下面這四個動詞是常見的「後面可接不定詞或動名詞但意義不同」的動詞：
(1) remember: (a) + V-ing ⇨ 記得做過…（事情已經做了）。
　　　　　　　 (b) + to V ⇨ 記得要做…，但是還沒做。
(2) forget: (a) + V-ing ⇨ 忘了已經做過…。
　　　　　　 (b) + to V ⇨ 忘了去做…（事情沒有做）。
(3) stop: (a) + V-ing ⇨ 停止做…。
　　　　　 (b) + to V ⇨ 停下來做…。
(4) regret: (a) + V-ing ⇨ 後悔做了…。
　　　　　　 (b) + to V ⇨ 遺憾要去做…。

Examples:

Remember:

(V-ing)   1. Jack remembered preparing food for his dog.

           (Jack 記得為狗準備食物了。) ⇨ 事情已做過，也記得。

(to V)   2. Jack remembered to prepare food for his dog.

           (Jack 記得要幫狗準備食物。) ⇨ 事情還沒做，但記得。

Forget:

(V-ing)   1. Serena forgot turning off the gas.

           (Serena 忘記已經關瓦斯了。) ⇨ 事情已做過，但忘記了。

(to V)   2. Serena forgot to turn off the gas.

           (Serena 忘了關瓦斯。) ⇨ 事情還沒做，也忘記要做。

Stop:

(V-ing)   1. Bill stopped crying when he saw his mother.

           (Bill 一看見媽媽就不哭了。) ⇨ 停止「哭」這個動作。

(to V)   2. Bill stopped to cry when he saw his mother.

           (Bill 看見媽媽就停下來大哭。) ⇨ 停止（走路）開始大哭。

Regret:

(V-ing)   1. She <u>regretted</u> <u>slapping</u> her boyfriend in public.

       （她很後悔當眾賞她男友耳光。）⇨後悔做過某事。

(to V)   2. I <u>regret</u> <u>to inform</u> you that your works are not accepted by our company.

       （我很遺憾地通知你，你的作品沒有被我們公司接受。）

請將括弧裡的動詞作適當變化，以完成句子。

1. It was lucky that Bill remembered _____ (*bring*) an umbrella with him. We didn't get wet.

2. I can't believe that you forgot _____ (*hand*) in your report. The teacher is very angry.

3. These two boys finally stopped _____ (*fight*) and made peace with each other.

4. Rita regretted _____ (*criticize*) her sister's dressing style after their quarrel.

5. Did you remember _____ (*return*) those VCDs to the rental store?

6. Kevin has totally forgotten _____ (*lock*) the door. His mother now can't get in the house after work.

7. Joe planned to study this afternoon, but when the earthquake hit, he stopped _____ (*run*) out of his room.

8. I regret _____ (*say*) that I have to refuse your gift.

四、常見含不定詞的句型

表「結果」
(1) too + Adj/Adv （＋ for 人/物）＋ to V ⇨ （對某人/物而言）太…而不能…
(2) Adj/Adv + enough （＋ for 人/物）＋ to V ⇨ （對某人/物而言）夠…而能做…
(3) so + Adj/Adv （＋for 人/物）＋ as to V ⇨ （對某人/物而言）如此…以致於…

Examples:

1. The weather is <u>too</u> hot <u>to</u> exercise outside.
   （天氣太熱，不能在戶外運動。）
2. The air is <u>too</u> dirty for us <u>to</u> breathe.
   （空氣髒到讓我們無法呼吸。）
3. The water is not warm <u>enough</u> <u>to</u> make tea.
   （水還沒熱到可以泡茶。）
4. This air conditioner is cheap <u>enough</u> <u>for everyone</u> <u>to</u> buy.
   （這台冷氣機便宜得每個人都可以購買。）
5. Harvey is <u>so</u> strong <u>as to</u> work for over 10 hours.
   （Harvey 壯得足以工作超過十小時。）

表「目的」：(in order) to V = (so as) to V ⇨ 為了…

Examples:

1. Emily studies hard <u>(in order) to</u> pass the final exam.
   （Emily 用功唸書，為了要通過期末考。）
2. Ben often eats lunch in that restaurant <u>(so as) to</u> make friends with the female clerk there.
   （因為要與那家餐廳的女店員交朋友，Ben 經常在那裡吃午餐。）

請依提示合併句子。

1. Betty is experienced.

   She can handle this difficult task.　　　　　　　(...*enough to*...)

   ⇨ _____

2. They were frightened.

   They couldn't describe what they saw.　　　　　(...*too...to*...)

   ⇨ _____

3. The little boy kept making loud noise.

   He wanted to watch cartoons.　　　　　　　　　(...*so as to*...)

   ⇨ _____

4. Elvira ran after George.

   She wanted to stop George from selling his house.　(*In order to*...)

   ⇨ _____

五、常見含動名詞的句型

一、表「禁止」: No + V-ing

Example:

Didn't you see the sign, which says "No smoking"?

（你沒看到那個牌子上寫著「禁止吸菸」嗎？）

二、從事某項活動：go + V-ing

Example:

Would you like to go roller-skating with us?

（你要不要和我們一起去溜冰？）

三、下面這些片語的後面一定要接動名詞：

(1) look forward to + V-ing ⇨ 期待…

(2) be/get used to + V-ing = be accustomed to + V-ing ⇨ 習慣於…

(3) be opposed to + V-ing = object to + V-ing ⇨ 反對…

(4) when it comes to + V-ing ⇨ 談到…

(5) It is no use + V-ing ⇨ …沒有用

(6) There is no + V-ing ⇨ …是不可能的

(7) come near to + V-ing ⇨ 幾乎…

(8) It is worth/worthwhile + V-ing ⇨ 值得…

(9) be busy + V-ing ⇨ 忙於…

(10) have a bad time + V-ing = have trouble + V-ing ⇨ …吃苦頭，…有困難

(11) cannot help + V-ing = cannot but + 原形 V ⇨ 不得不…，忍不住…

Examples:

<< 期待 >> We look forward to visiting you this summer.

（我們期待今夏去拜訪你。）

<< 習慣於 >>　After practice, Helen has gotten used to milking the cows.

　　　　　= After practice, Helen has been accustomed to milking the cows.

　　　　　（經過練習後，Helen 已習慣擠牛奶了。）

<< 反對 >>　Mike was firmly opposed to taking medicine before sleeping.

　　　　　= Mike firmly objected to taking medicine before sleeping.

　　　　　（Mike 堅決反對睡覺前吃藥。）

<< 談到 >>　When it comes to cooking, no one in this neighborhood is better than my mother.

　　　　　（談到烹飪，這附近沒有人比我媽媽好。）

<< 沒有用 >>　It is no use shouting at that bad guy. You should try another way to defeat him.

　　　　　（向這個壞蛋吼叫一點用也沒有，你該試試其他方法來打敗他。）

<< 不可能 >>　There is no telling when the rain will stop.

　　　　　（很難說雨何時會停。）

<< 幾乎 >>　Watch out! The car came near to hitting you.

　　　　　（小心！那部車幾乎撞到你了。）

<< 值得 >>　Books written by famous writers are all worth reading.

　　　　　= It is worthwhile reading books written by famous writers.

　　　　　（知名作家所寫的書都很值得一讀。）

<< 忙於 >>　Don't bother John. He is busy writing an important article.

　　　　　（別去打擾 John，他正忙著寫一篇很重要的文章。）

<< 有困難 >>　They knew that he had a bad time making a speech on stage.

　　　　　= They knew that he had trouble making a speech on stage.

　　　　　（他們知道他上臺演說有困難。）

<< 不得不 >>　When hearing the bad news, Kenneth cannot help crying sadly.

　　　　　（當聽到這壞消息時，Kenneth 忍不住傷心地哭了。）

Try This !

I. 請將括弧裡的動詞作適當變化，以完成句子。

1. When Laura plays the violin, no _____ (*talk*) is allowed.

2. I'm looking forward to _____ (*hear*) from you soon.

3. In the speech contest, she came near to _____ (*defeat*) her opponents.

4. On the weekend, many people go _____ (*jog*) in the park.

5. Remember that it is no use _____ (*cry*) over spilt milk.

6. In these days, I have been accustomed to _____ (*live*) in this big city.

7. The farmers strongly objected to _____ (*build*) a power plant near their houses.

8. When it comes to _____ (*sing*), he becomes excited.

9. I'm sorry that I can't talk to you now. I'm busy _____ (*look*) for some data.

10. In this hot day, Douglas cannot help _____ (*eat*) a lot of ice cream.

II. 根據中文完成英文句子。

1. 雖然你犯了點錯，你的誠實值得鼓勵。

Although you made some mistakes, your honesty was _____ _____ .

2. 如果我知道你慢跑有困難，我就不會要你參加比賽了。

If I had known you had _____ _____ , I wouldn't have asked you to join this contest.

3. Morgan 已經幾乎要放棄自己了。我們得幫幫他。

Morgan has _____ _____ _____ _____ up himself. We have to help him.

4. 好幾天不能出去玩，小孩們都忍不住在抱怨雨天。

The children cannot help _____ about the rainy days because of not being able to go out to play for so many days.

六、不定詞或動名詞作主詞，與虛主詞 it 互換的句型

以不定詞或動名詞作主詞時，有時主詞較長，此時我們可以：

(1) 用 it 作虛主詞，把真主詞後移，

(2) 真主詞要改為不定詞的形式。

句型：To V_1/V_1-ing + be/V_2…. = It + be/V_2… + to V_1….

Examples:（劃底線部份表示真主詞）

1. To do two things at the same time is very difficult.
   = It is very difficult to do two things at the same time.
   （同時做兩件事情是非常困難的。）

2. To sail across the Pacific Ocean took them two weeks.
   = It took them two weeks to sail across the Pacific Ocean.
   （航行橫越太平洋花了他們兩週的時間。）

3. Traveling alone in Africa made him more mature than before.
   = It made him more mature than before to travel alone in Africa.
   （獨自到非洲旅行讓他比以前成熟許多。）⇨真主詞部份改以不定詞 to travel… 形式。

4. Is riding a horse easy?
   = Is it easy to ride a horse?
   （騎馬容易嗎？）⇨真主詞部份改以不定詞 to ride… 的形式。

Try This !

請將下面的句子改寫為以虛主詞 it 起首的句子。

1. Is taking a long walk relaxing?

   ⇨ _____

2. To take a bus to work may take more time.

   ⇨ _____

3. Reading more classics can enrich our mind.

   ⇨ _____

4. Does making good friends take long time?

   ⇨ _____

7-2 分詞

現在分詞 V-ing	1. 代表意義：動作是主動或持續中
	2. 形成時態：進行式
	3. 形成語態：主動語態
	4. 當形容詞時，表示「令人…的」，亦即通常用來修飾物或事件
過去分詞 PP	1. 代表意義：動作是被動、已完成或結束
	2. 形成時態：完成式
	3. 形成語態：被動語態
	4. 當形容詞用來修飾人時，表示「感到…」

Examples:

<< 現在分詞 >>　1. Jonnie saw the man crossing the bridge.

（Jonnie 看到那個男人過了橋樑。）

2. When I called, Mary was preparing dinner.

（當我打電話過去時，Mary 正在準備晚餐。）

3. My father sat there saying nothing.

（我爸爸坐在那裡一言不發。）

4. It is amazing for him to be elected as the class leader.

（他被選為班長，真是令人驚訝。）

<< 過去分詞 >>　1. Pan was cheated by David.

（Pan 被 David 給騙了。）

2. We found a little girl deserted on the corner of the street.

（我們發現一個小女孩被遺棄在街角。）

3. All the kids are excited to see Uncle McDonald.

（所有的小孩看到麥當勞叔叔都很興奮。）

請圈選出符合句意的分詞。

1. Gina felt (embarrassed/embarrassing) when we looked at her pictures of childhood.

2. My sister was (enjoyed/enjoying) ice cream when we opened her door.

3. Tom was (punished/punishing) because he broke our neighbor's window.

4. I came home to find my dinner (eating/eaten) by someone.

5. The young man was seen (robbing/robbed) an old lady in front of the bank.

6. It is (bored/boring) to watch the same movie over and over again.

7. Watch out! There is (breaking/broken) glass all over the ground.

8. Those (frightening/frightened) masks should be hidden away from children.

9. My father sat there (staring/stared) at me, (saying/said) nothing.

10. I don't know why the food is left (untouched/untouching).

7–3 分詞構句與分詞片語

分詞構句主要是由從屬子句、對等子句或關係子句簡化而來。在從屬子句與對等子句裡，只要從屬子句與對等子句的主詞與主要子句相同時，就可以寫成分詞構句；而關係子句簡化而來的分詞片語，則是關代為主格時的省略。

表「時間」的從屬子句：

(1) 從屬連接詞 before, after：before, after 可以省略，句型如下：

After/Before + S_1 + V_1, S_1 + V_2 = V_1-ing, S_1 + V_2

(2) 從屬連接詞 when, as: when, as 可以省略，句型如下：

When/As + S_1 + V_1, S_1 + V_2

= When/As V_1-ing, S_1 + V_2 = V_1-ing, S_1 + V_2

Examples:

1. After I finished my homework, I went to bed.

   = Finishing my homework, I went to bed.

   （做完功課後我就去睡覺了。）

2. As we arrived at home this evening, we found someone breaking into our house.

   = Arriving at home this evening, we found someone breaking into our house.

   （今天傍晚到家時，我們發現有人闖入家裡。）

表「理由、原因」的從屬子句

省略連接詞 because, so, as, since 等，句型如下：

Because/So/As/Since + S_1 + V_1, S_1 + V_2 = V_1-ing, S_1 + V_2

Examples:

1. Because they didn't know where their son was, they turned to the police for help.

   = Not knowing where their son was, they turned to the police for help.

   （因為不知道他們的兒子在哪裡，他們向警方求助。）⇨否定的 not 須保留。

2. Since you broke the cup, you should buy a new one.

    = Breaking the cup, you should buy a new one.

    （既然你打破了杯子，你就該去買個新的。）

表「附帶條件或狀況」的對等子句

省略對等連接詞 and，被省略的子句是用來表達「附帶條件或狀況」。句型如下：

$S_1 + V_1$, and $S_1 + V_2 = S_1 + V_1$, V_2-ing

Examples:

1. Joseph walked into the classroom, and he slammed the door loudly.

    ⇨ Joseph walked into the classroom, slamming the door loudly.

    （Joseph 走進教室，大聲的把門關上。）

2. He threatened to break everything in the house, and he waved his fists at us.

    ⇨ He threatened to break everything in the house, waving his fists at us.

    （他威脅破壞房子裡所有的東西，還對著我們揮拳頭。）

請將下列句子劃線部分改寫為分詞構句。

1. As she was too tired, she rested her head on my shoulder to take a rest.

    ⇨ _____

2. Maria sat on the sofa, and read stories to her children.

    ⇨ _____

3. After they finished their final exam, all the students cried out loudly and jumped around happily.

    ⇨ _____

4. Lisa slept in her room, and snored loudly.

    ⇨ _____

關係子句簡化而來的分詞片語，屬於關代為主格 (who, which, that) 時的省略，且為限定：

(1) 關係子句動詞為 be 動詞時，可直接將關代與 be 動詞省略。

先行詞 + who/which/that + be V-ing/PP/片語 ...

= 先行詞 + V-ing/PP/片語 ...

(2) 關係子句動詞為一般動詞時，句型如下：

先行詞 + who/which/that + V …

= 先行詞 + V-ing …

(3) 關係子句為 have/has + PP 時，句型如下：

先行詞 + who/which/that + have/has + PP...

= 先行詞 + having + PP...

Examples:

<<be 動詞>>   1. Who is the girl that is playing the guitar?

= Who is the girl playing the guitar?

（那位在彈吉他的女孩是誰啊？） ⇨ that is 省略

2. The policeman who was writing a report at 10:00 last night is my father.

= The policeman writing a report at 10:00 last night is my father.

（昨晚十點時正在寫報告的警察是我父親。） ⇨ who was 省略

3. The tree which was cut down by that boy is a cherry tree.

= The tree cut down by that boy is a cherry tree.

（被那個男孩砍倒的樹是株櫻桃樹。） ⇨ which was 省略

4. The benches which are in the park are green.

= The benches in the park are green.

（公園裡的長椅是綠色的。） ⇨ which are 省略

<< 一般動詞 >> 1. The man who sits in front of you is our boss.

= The man sitting in front of you is our boss.

（坐在你前面的男人是我們的老闆。）

⇨省略 who，一般動詞 sits 改為 sitting。

2. The dog <u>which sleeps peacefully</u> is Ted's pet.

 = The dog <u>sleeping peacefully</u> is Ted's pet.

 （那隻安靜睡覺的狗是 Ted 的寵物。）

 ⇨省略 which，一般動詞 sleeps 改為 sleeping。

<<have/has + PP>> 1. My student <u>who has won the race</u> comes from a poor family.

 = My student <u>having won the race</u> comes from a poor family.

 （我那位剛贏得比賽的學生來自一個貧窮的家庭。）

 ⇨省略 who，has 改為 having。

2. The girl <u>who has been punished by Mr. Wong</u> is Mark's sister.

 = The girl <u>having been punished by Mr. Wong</u> is Mark's sister.

 （那個剛剛被王先生處罰的女孩是 Mark 的妹妹。）

 ⇨省略 who，has 改為 having。

注意 請務必小心比較上面所有例句的時態與語態，以舉一反三！

分詞構句的注意事項：

(1) 分詞構句中，過去分詞前的 being 或 having been 是可以一併省略的；

(2) 分詞構句中，可以省略的連接詞如 when, before, after 等，有時會保留，使句意更清楚。

Examples:

1. As he was fired by his company, he couldn't support his family anymore.

 = <u>Being fired by his company,</u> he couldn't support his family anymore.

 = <u>Fired by his company,</u> he couldn't support his family anymore.

 （因為被公司開除，他無法養家活口了。）

2. When I discussed my future plan with my professor, I told him that I wanted to major in computer engineering.

 = <u>Discussing my future plan with my professor,</u> I told him that I wanted to major in computer engineering.

 = <u>When discussing my future plan with my professor,</u> I told him that I wanted to major in computer engineering.

 （在與教授討論我未來的計畫時，我告訴他我要主修電腦工程。）

請將下列句子劃線部份改寫為分詞構句或分詞片語。

1. The woman who was blamed for her being unfriendly has two children.

   ⇨ _____

2. The train which has been crowded with people is destined for Taichung.

   ⇨ _____

3. The plane that is filled with rice and vegetable is going to take off.

   ⇨ _____

4. The factory which has opened for more than 20 years produces chips.

   ⇨ _____

5. As Joseph caught a cold, he couldn't join the party last night.

   ⇨ _____

6. When he is compared with his brother, he is considered to be more cunning.

   ⇨ _____

I. 選出正確的答案。

1. A stranger came up to me, _____ if I could lend him some money to take a bus.

(A) ask　　　(B) asking　　　(C) asked　　　(D) to ask

2. They try to persuade her _____ so much money on clothes.

(A) not to spend　(B) to not spend　(C) not spending　(D) spending not

3. The typhoon came near to _____ all the grapes.

(A) destroy　　(B) destroying　　(C) to destroy　　(D) be destroyed

4. _____ well, Jessie decided to take a day off to stay at home.

(A) Not feeling　(B) Not to feel　(C) Feeling not　(D) To feel

5. It is agreed that there is no _____ for taste.

(A) account　　(B) to account　　(C) to accounting　(D) accounting

6. One of a mother's greatest concerns toward her children is to offer them delicious food _____ them healthy.

(A) make　　(B) made　　(C) to make　　(D) making

7. There is something wrong with your car. You had better have it _____ .

(A) fix　　(B) fixing　　(C) fixed　　(D) to fix

8. Most students prefer surfing on the Internet to _____ to school for education.

(A) go　　(B) going　　(C) gone　　(D) have gone

9. Tom Cruise reveals that he has trouble _____ even after he has grown up.

(A) reading　　(B) to read　　(C) read　　(D) to reading

10. The story is about a husband _____ by his wife when she found out his affair with another woman.

(A) who killed　(B) who killing　(C) killing　(D) killed

11. As we were walking in the woods, we found a house _____ by huge tree roots.

(A) destroy　　(B) destroying　　(C) destroyed　　(D) to destroy

12. To set up a date for him _____ a lot of time.

(A) is (B) has (C) takes (D) making

II. 完成下列代換句。

13. It is impossible for me to sleep 2 hours a day.

= _____ _____ 2 hours a day _____ _____ for me.

14. I almost forget that I have talked to that person before.

= I almost forget _____ _____ to that person before.

15. My grandparents were glad that we visited them last weekend.

= My grandparents were glad of our _____ them last weekend.

16. Hearing her tragedy, we couldn't help weeping for her.

= Hearing her tragedy, we couldn't but _____ for her.

17. He gets up early every morning because he wants to catch the first train.

= He gets up early every morning _____ _____ _____ catch the first train.

18. You are so nice to help me with my homework.

= It is so _____ of you to help me with my homework.

III. 挑錯並改正。

( ) _____ 19. (A)Though (B)regret (C)misunderstanding her children, the mother refused (D)to say sorry first.

( ) _____ 20. (A)To making our environment (B)better, the government demand all citizens (C)to recycle plastics and (D)reuse paper.

( ) _____ 21. What I want (A)to do as my lifelong career is to (B)setting up an orphanage (C)to take care of those (D)deserted children.

( ) _____ 22. Mike is (A)such an honest (B)that I have never (C)heard him (D)speaking ill of others.

IV. 填充式翻譯。

23. 談到慢跑時，沒有人會是 Harvey 的對手。

When it _____ _____ _____, no one is able to beat Harvey.

24. 因為不知道身在何處，我們停下車來問路。·

_____ _____ where we were, we stopped _____ _____ for directions.

25. 吃完午餐的學生可以先吃水果。

The students _____ _____ their lunch _____ _____ fruit first.

26. 活到老學到老。

One is never _____ old _____ learn.

27. 說是一回事，做又是另一回事。

_____ _____ is one thing; _____ _____ is another.

28. 這件牛仔褲一點也不值得買。

This pair of jeans is not _____ _____ at all.

Chapter 8 　　形容詞、副詞與級的用法

在英文子句中，形容詞與副詞都是扮演修飾的角色。形容詞用來修飾名詞與代名詞；副詞修飾動詞、形容詞、副詞本身，或整個句子。

8-1　形容詞的種類與用法

指示形容詞	包括 this, that, these, those
數量形容詞	(1) 基數，如 one, two, three, ... (2) 其餘數量的形容詞包括 some, any, few, little, a lot, many, much, several, a number of...
性狀形容詞	(1) 包括 good, old, wooden 等許多的形容詞。 (2) 常見的字尾有 -ful, -al, -tive, -ic, -ish, -ous, -able, -ible, -y, -or, -ant, -en, -ing, -ed 等等。 (3) 使用兩個以上的性狀形容詞，要注意以下的排列順序： 　（大小─年齡─形狀─顏色─血統（國籍）─來源─材料成分─用途） 　＋名詞
疑問形容詞	包括 what, which, whose
形容詞片語	有下列三種情況： (1) 介系詞片語當形容詞用：N + 介系詞片語 (2) 分詞片語當形容詞用：N + V-ing/PP (3) 不定詞片語當形容詞用：N + to V
形容詞子句	就是我們在第六章所學到的關係子句。

Examples:

<< 指示形容詞 >> 　Who put <u>that</u> magazine on my desk?
　　　　　　　　　（誰把那本雜誌放在我桌上？）

<< 數量形容詞 >> 　Helen invited <u>several</u> friends to her place.
　　　　　　　　　（Helen 邀了幾個朋友到她家。）

<< 性狀形容詞 >> 　Jenny wears a <u>long</u>, <u>black</u>, <u>leather</u> skirt.
　　　　　　　　　（Jenny 穿件黑色的長皮裙。）

<< 疑問形容詞 >> 　<u>Which</u> glass is yours?
　　　　　　　　　（哪個杯子是你的？）

<< 形容詞片語 >>　　Do you need a pen <u>to write with</u>?

（你需要一支筆寫字嗎？）

Try This !

請將下面的字重新組合。

1. a / large / bookcase / wooden / Italian ⇨ _____

2. an / expensive / hanger / clothes ⇨ _____

3. a / tall / young / lady / beautiful ⇨ _____

4. a / fat / bird / gray / small ⇨ _____

5. a / orange / huge / sweet ⇨ _____

8-2 副詞的種類與用法

情狀副詞	well, badly, gently, angrily..., 通常是情狀形容詞加 ly 形成。
時間副詞	today, tomorrow, on Monday, this Saturday, next year...
頻率副詞	always, often, frequently, usually, sometimes, seldom, rare, never
程度副詞	very, much, little, too, enough, hardly, nearly, almost, quite...
地方副詞	here, there, inside, outside, in the bedroom, in Taiwan...
疑問副詞	就是 wh- 疑問詞：where, how, why, when
關係副詞	when, where, why, how
修飾全句的副詞	除部分情狀副詞外，還包括轉折詞：however, as a result, besides, likewise...
表肯定或否定的副詞	yes, no, not...，其中 no 又常跟比較級連用形成片語：no less than, no more than...

Examples:

<< 情狀副詞 >> I didn't do anything wrong, but my teacher looked at me angrily.
（我沒做錯事，老師卻生氣的看著我。）

<< 時間副詞 >> They go to church on Sundays.
（他們每週日上教堂。）

<< 頻率副詞 >> Jack seldom plays online games.
（Jack 很少玩線上遊戲。）

<< 程度副詞 >> My father was very busy these days, so we didn't see him much.
（我的父親這幾天非常忙碌，所以我們很少看到他）

<< 地方副詞 >> Mary is not here. She might be in the bedroom.
（Mary 不在這裡，她可能在臥室。）

<< 疑問副詞 >> When was the last time you saw John?
（你最後一次看到 John 是什麼時候？）

<< 關係副詞 >>	No one knows the reason <u>why</u> the test is cancelled.
	（沒有人知道為什麼考試會取消。）
<< 修飾全句副詞 >>	Helen is not the best student in my class. <u>However</u>, she is the most diligent one.
	（Helen 不是我班上最好的學生，然而，她是最努力的一位。）
<< 表肯定否定副詞 >>	I have <u>no more than</u> 1,000 dollars with me.
	（我身上的錢不超過一千元。）

請根據句意，圈選出適當的副詞。

1. He sang the song (terrible, terribly, terriblely).

2. It's so hot that we have to concentrate (hard, hardly) on our studying.

3. (Unfortunate, Unfortunately), we lost two great pilots in the air crash.

4. We (sometime, sometimes, some time) watch horror movies at midnight.

5. Could you show me the way (what, how, which) you solve this math question?

6. My mother was cooking (busy, busily, busier) in the kitchen.

7. Vincent will give me his violin (yesterday, last year, tomorrow).

8. Lily doesn't like spicy food, so she (hardly, almost, much) go to a Si-chuan restaurant.

9. Ted locked the door from the (inside, beside), so you couldn't open the door.

10. (How, When, Why) will we go to Japan, by boat or by plane?

8–3 原級、比較級與最高級—基本句型

一、原級的基本句型

原級的基本句型：
S_1 + be/V + as Adj/Adv as + S_2
否定的句型：
S_1 + ...not + as Adj/Adv as + S_2
= S_1 + ...not + so Adj/Adv as + S_2

Examples:

1. Tina is <u>as old as</u> Sam. (Tina 的年紀和 Sam 一樣大。)
2. Maggie runs <u>as slowly as</u> a turtle. (Maggie 跑得非常慢。)
3. Judy is <u>not as clever as</u> her sister. (Judy 沒有她姊姊來得聰明。)
   = Judy is <u>not so clever as</u> her sister.

原級前面可以接以下的副詞修飾：
almost, nearly, just, quite, exactly, about, every bit

Examples:

1. Your dress is <u>almost</u> <u>as cheap as</u> mine. (你的衣服幾乎和我的一樣便宜。)
2. Martha can swim <u>nearly</u> <u>as fast as</u> a shark. (Martha 可以游得差不多跟鯊魚一樣快)

原級的慣用語：
(1) 一樣多：as many + 複數名詞 + as
　　　　　　 as much + 不可數名詞 + as
(2) 盡可能：as Adj/Adv as possible
　　　　　　 = as Adj/Adv as one can

Examples:

<< 一樣多 >>　　1. Elves has <u>as many clothes as</u> I.

　　　　　　　　　（Elves 的衣服和我的一樣多。）

　　　　　　　2. Linda drinks <u>as much water as</u> fish during the competition.

　　　　　　　　　（Linda 在比賽中狂喝水。）

<< 盡可能 >>　　1. I need you right away! Please come <u>as soon as possible.</u>

　　　　　　　　　（我現在就需要你！請你盡可能快點過來。）

　　　　　　　2. Tina has to study <u>as hard as she can</u>, or she might be flunked.

　　　　　　　　　（Tina 必須盡可能的用功，否則她有可能會被當掉。）

Try This !

I. 請依提示改寫句子。

1. My grandfather goes to bed early, and my grandmother goes to bed early, too.

　　　　　　　　　　　　　　　　　　　　　　　(*as...as*)

　　⇨ _____

2. Mike has only one car whereas Jim has four cars.　　(*not so...as*)

　　⇨ _____

3. He tried to finish the work quickly.　　　　　　(*as...as possible*)

　　⇨ _____

4. Joe owns two houses, and Dick owns two houses, too.　(*as many ... as*)

　　⇨ _____

5. I can't work any faster.　　　　　　　　　　(*as....as one can*)

　　⇨ _____

II. 根據中文完成英文句子。

1. 我希望有一天我打籃球能打得像 Michael Jordan 一樣好。

　I wish that I could play basketball _____ _____

　_____ Michael Jordan one day.

2. 在我看來，莫札特與巴哈一樣偉大。

　In my opinion, Mozart is _____ _____ _____ J.S. Bach.

二、比較級的基本句型

> 比較級的基本句型：
> (1)「優等」比較：S_1... Adj-er (+ N)/Adv-er 或 more Adj/Adv + than S_2
> (2)「劣等」比較：S_1... less Adj/Adv + than S_2

Examples:

1. He always gives <u>better</u> performance in art <u>than</u> I (do). （他在藝術上的表現總是比我好。）
2. Judy is <u>less popular than</u> her sister. （Judy 沒有她姊姊那麼受歡迎。）

> 比較級前面可以接以下的副詞修飾：
> much, a lot, a little, far...

Example:

Tom looks <u>a little</u> <u>older than</u> he is. （Tom 看起來比實際年齡老一點。）

> 下面幾個片語帶有比較級的涵義：
> be superior to（較優秀） be inferior to（較差）
> be senior to（較年長） be junior to（較年輕）

Examples:

1. Ann always feels that she <u>is inferior to</u> others. （Ann 總是覺得自己不如他人。）
2. Louis <u>is junior to</u> Harvey. （Louis 比 Harvey 年輕。）

> 表示「越來越」、「漸漸的」的句型：
> S + be/V + ～er and ～er 或 more and more ～

Examples:

1. The weather is getting <u>hotter and hotter</u>. （天氣漸漸地熱了。）
2. He is tired. He walks <u>more and more slowly</u>. （他累了，走得越來越慢。）

I. 請依提示合併或改寫句子。

1. My cousin is not as handsome as I.　　　　　　　　　　　　　（劣等比較）
　⇨ _____

2. Ray is twelve years old and I am twenty years old. (*A: be junior to; B:* 優等比較)
　⇨ A = _____
　⇨ B = _____

3. ⎰I get up at 6:30 in the morning.
　 ⎱Tina gets up at 7:00 in the morning.　　　　　　　　　（優等比較）
　⇨ _____

II. 根據中文完成英文句子。

1. 這棟大樓比我家的公寓要高得多。
　This building is _____ _____ than my apartment.

2. Amy 隨著年齡的增長，變得越來越漂亮了。
　Amy became _____ _____ _____ _____ as she grew up.

3. Fred 的英語總是比別人好。
　Fred's English is always _____ to others.
　= Fred's English is always _____ _____ others

三、最高級的基本句型

最高級的基本句型：
(1)「優等」比較：S + be/V + the ～est 或 the most ～
(2)「劣等」比較：S + be/V + the least ～

Examples:

1. Uncle Tom is the richest in our family.
   （Tom 叔叔是我們家族裡最有錢的。）
2. He is the least person that I want to see.
   （他是我最不想見到的人。）

最高級前面可以接以下的副詞修飾：
very, much, by far 等，其中 "very" 要放在 the 和形容詞之間。

Example:

She is by far the kindest person I know.
（她是我目前我所認識最仁慈的人。）

表示「三者中最…」、「全體中最…」的句型：
(1) 三者中最…：S + be/V + the ～est 或 the most ～ + of the three + N
(2) 全體中最…：S + be/V + the ～est 或 the most ～ + of all the + N

Examples:

1. Allan is the youngest of all the classmates.
   （Allan 是他的同學中最年輕的。）
2. Judy is the most successful of the three good friends.
   （Judy 是三位好朋友中最成功的一位。）

最高級常用的兩個應用句：
(1) 所曾經做過或看過最⋯的：
    S + be/V + the ~est 或 the most ~ + N（單數）+ that + S + have/has + PP
    S + be/V + the ~est 或 the most ~ + N（單數）+ that + 子句
(2) 最⋯的人之一：
    S + be/V + one of + the ~est 或 the most ~ + N（複數）+ 介系詞片語

Ⓔxamples:

1. This is the best movie that I have ever seen.
    （這是我所看過最棒的電影。）
2. The computer is the most powerful calculator that we have in the world.
    （電腦是世界上我們所擁有運算能力最強大的計算機。）
3. My brother is one of the most active students in our school.
    （我哥哥是我們學校裡最活躍的學生之一。）

I. 請依提示改寫句子。

1. I've seen the movie, but it is terribly boring.（請用最高級 + *that...ever* 合併兩句）
    ⇨ _____
2. Camping in the mountains was a very bad experience in my life.
                             （用 *one of the ~est* 改寫）
    ⇨ _____
3. No other magazine in this bookstore is so attracting as *Time*.   （*the ~est*）
    ⇨ _____

II. 根據中文完成英文句子。

1. Linda 是我所見過最有自信的人。
    Linda is _____ _____ _____ person that I have ever seen.
2. 連最強壯的人也抬不起這塊石頭。
    Even _____ _____ person can't lift this stone.
3. 這個人是全辦公室裡最懶的人！
    This man is _____ _____ diligent in the office!

8–4　原級、比較級與最高級─變化句型

一、以原級與比較級的型態來表達最高級的重要句型

以原級表達最高級的重要句型：

S + be/V + the ~est/the most ~

= Nothing/Nobody/No other 單數名詞 + be/V + so/as + 原級 + as S

Examples:

1. Taipei is <u>the biggest city</u> in Taiwan.

    = <u>No other city</u> in Taiwan is <u>as big as</u> Taipei.

    （臺北是臺灣最大的城市。）

2. Michael Jordan <u>plays basketball the best</u> in the world.

    = <u>Nobody</u> in the world <u>plays basketball so well as</u> Michael Jordan.

    （在這個世界上，沒有人籃球打得比 Michael Jordan 好。）

以比較級表達最高級的重要句型：

S + be/V + the ~est 或 the most ~

= S + be/V + ~er 或 more ~ + than + any other 單數名詞

　　　　　　　　　　　　　　　　　　all the other 複數名詞

= Nothing/Nobody/No other 單數名詞 + be/V + ~er 或 more ~ + than....

Examples:

1. She dances <u>the most gracefully</u> in her class.

    = She dances <u>more gracefully than any other girl</u> in her class.

    = She dances <u>more gracefully than all the other girls</u> in her class.

    = <u>No other girl</u> in her class dances <u>more gracefully</u> than she.

    （在她的班上，她跳舞最優雅。）

2. He is the rudest boy in his class.

    = He is ruder than any other boy in his class.

    = He is ruder than all the other boys in his class.

    = No other boy in his class is ruder than he.

    （他在他們班上是最粗魯的男生。）

二、其他變化句型

「多少倍⋯」的句型 ⇨ 原級的變化句型

S_1 + be/V + 倍數 + as Adj/Adv + as S_2

= S_1 + be/V + 倍數 + the + N + of S_2

Example:

    This box is three times as heavy as that one (is).

    = This box is three times the weight of that one.

    （這個箱子是那個的三倍重。）

「兩個之中較⋯」的句型 ⇨ 比較級的變化句型：

S + be/V + the ～er 或 the more ～ of the two....

Example:

    Jacky is the taller of the two boys.

    （Jacky 是這兩個男孩中較高的。）

雙重比較：「越⋯就越⋯」的句型 ⇨ 比較級的變化句型

    The ～er/more ～ + S + V, the ～er/more ～ + S + V

Example:

    The more quickly you walk, the warmer you feel.

    （你走得越快，就越覺得溫暖。）

請依提示改寫句子。

1. She is the most diligent student in our class.

(*A: ...more...than any other; B: No other...than....*)

➡ A = _____

➡ B = _____

2. Making money is the most important thing to Jack. (*Nothing...as important as....*)

➡ _____

3. My sister's CDs are twice as many as mine. (*twice the...of...*)

➡ _____

4. Lisa is 28 years old, and Tina is 30 years old. (*...of the two women*)

➡ _____

5. If you smoke less, you will be more healthy. (*The less..., the more....*)

➡ _____

6. No other student in my class sings so beautifully as Maria.

(*Maria...more...than all the other....*)

➡ _____

7. Tim drives the most safely among us. (*Nobody...more...than....*)

➡ _____

I. 選出正確的答案。

1. _____ speaking, you don't look good in your wedding dress.
   (A) Frank   (B) Frankly   (C) Honesty   (D) More honest

2. Parents all want their children to study _____ .
   (A) very hardly   (B) much hard   (C) enough hardly   (D) hard

3. We finally figure out _____ Bill Gates becomes such a successful businessman.
   (A) how   (B) where   (C) why   (D) what

4. The United States has more powerful weapons than _____ in the world.
   (A) all the countries   (B) all the other countries
   (C) any other countries   (D) the all countries

5. You should prepare yourself against your enemy as _____ .
   (A) possible as you can   (B) possible as you do
   (C) well as it's possible   (D) as good as possible

6. That boy's hair is _____ mine.
   (A) as twice as long   (B) as long twice as
   (C) twice as long as   (D) long as twice as

7. The road is _____ for two cars to pass.
   (A) too wide   (B) enough wide   (C) wide enough   (D) narrow

8. The more you learn, the more _____ you will become ahead of others.
   (A) easily   (B) easy   (C) easiness   (D) ease

9. Kenting is _____ the most popular tourist spot in Taiwan.
   (A) yet   (B) by far   (C) even   (D) quite

10. We all know that trains run _____ than cars.
    (A) very faster   (B) more fast   (C) more fastly   (D) much faster

11. Quitting from school is _____ decision he has ever made.
    (A) bad   (B) worse   (C) the worst   (D) the badest

12. How _____ do your parents go on a vacation?
    (A) long   (B) often   (C) soon   (D) usually

II. 代換，等式後的句子意義需完全相同。

13. Maria has twenty cousins and I have two.

    = Maria has _____ _____ the number of cousins _____ I do.

14. July and August are hotter than any other month in Taiwan.

    = July and August are _____ _____ of all the twelve months in Taiwan.

15. Hip hop is the most attractive music to me.

    = Hip hop is _____ _____ than _____ music to me.

    = No other music is _____ _____ as Hip hop to me.

III. 挑錯並改正。

(   ) _____ 16. (A)When carrying out the plan, we found (B)it (C)difficulty to deal with the (D)matter of money.

(   ) _____ 17. In the old (A)times, people had wanted to fly (B)highly in the sky. That's (C)why airplanes (D)were invented.

(   ) _____ 18. (A)Look at your mother. She looks (B)at least (C)twice (D)young than she actually is.

(   ) _____ 19. Sally is (A)the much (B)most brilliant worker that (C)most companies want to (D)hire.

(   ) _____ 20. New York is (A)much (B)larger than (C)any other (D)cities in U.S.

IV. 根據中文完成英文句子。

21. 人生沒有比失去摯愛的家人更糟的事了。

    There is nothing _____ _____ losing one's beloved family members.

22. 隨著網際網路的發明，資訊的取得越來越快速且容易。

    With the invention of the Internet, obtaining information is getting _____ and _____ .

23. 他是臺灣最紅的演員之一。

    He is _____ _____ _____ actors in Taiwan.

24. John 常運動，這也是為什麼他會強壯如牛的原因。

John exercises a lot, and that's why he is _____ _____ _____

an ox.

25. 擁有越多，慾望越多。

_____ _____ one   owns, _____ _____ one

desires.

26. 這個團體裡沒有第二個人跟他一樣幽默了。

_____ in this group is _____ humorous _____ he.

= He is _____ _____ than _____ _____ _____

members in this group.

Chapter 9 連接詞

所謂的連接詞是可以用來連接單字、片語、子句或句子的單字或詞組。依照功能，可以分為對等連接詞、從屬連接詞與準連接詞。

 9-1 對等連接詞

對等連接詞有兩類—單字型與片語型，說明如下：

一、單字型的對等連接詞有：

and（而且），but（但是），or（或，否則），nor（也不），neither（也不），so（所以），yet（但是），for（因為）

在這之中，so、yet 與 for 只接子句，其餘則可連接單字、片語、子句或句子。

Examples:

1. They didn't order pizza, <u>nor</u> did we.
   （他們沒有訂披薩，我們也沒有。）
2. Sally doesn't tell a lie, <u>neither</u> do we.
   （Sally 沒有說謊，我們也沒有。）
3. Tom studied hard for the exam, <u>yet</u> he still failed.
   （Tom 為了考試很用功地唸書，但他還是不及格。）
4. Mike didn't go to work today, <u>for</u> an accident happened to his mother.
   （Mike 今天沒來上班，因為他媽媽發生意外。）

二、片語型的對等連接詞在連接主詞時，要注意主詞與動詞的一致：

(1) both A and B ⇨ 「A 與 B 兩者都…」，動詞複數。

(2) either A or B ⇨ 「不是 A 就是 B…」，動詞與 B 一致。

(3) neither A nor B ⇨ 「既不是 A 也不是 B…」，動詞與 B 一致。

(4) not only A but also B ⇨ 「不只 A，還有 B…」，動詞與 B 一致

   = A as well as B ⇨ 此時動詞與 A 一致。

Examples:

1. <u>Both</u> John <u>and</u> Mary <u>are</u> my good friends.
   （John 與 Mary 都是我的好朋友。）

2. Either Tom or I have to change the baby's diaper.
（不是 Tom 就是我必須替嬰兒換尿布。）

3. I believe neither that John is a gay nor that he likes Barbara Streisand.
（我不相信 John 是同性戀，也不相信他喜歡 Barbara Streisand。）⇨ A、B 皆為 that 子句

4. Not only Claire but also I like to listen to opera.
　= Claire as well as I likes to listen to opera.
（不只 Claire 還有我都喜歡聽歌劇。）

5. Not only you but also Richard made the same mistake.
（你與 Richard 都犯了相同的錯誤。）

Try This !

I. 從對等連接詞 and, but, or, nor, so, yet, for 中選出適當者填入句中。

1. Be polite to them, _____ they are our important customers.

2. Plastic bottles are not good to our environment, _____ people have to recycle them.

3. Work hard, _____ you will make more money and get promotion.

4. Work hard, _____ you won't make enough money to support the family.

5. He is not handsome _____ gentle to people.

6. It is getting cold these days, _____ you had better wear a jacket when you go out.

7. What do you prefer, coffee _____ tea?

8. He promised to come to the party, _____ we haven't seen him yet.

II. 請依提示合併句子。

1. You are to blame for the fault.
　John is to blame for the fault.　　　　　　　　　　(either...or...)
　⇨ _____

2. Elsa is good at singing.
　Elsa is good at composing, too.　　　　　　　　　　(...as well as...)
　⇨ _____

3. Martha didn't know what to do.
　Alice didn't know what to do, either.　　　　　　　　(Neither...nor....)
　⇨ _____

9-2 從屬連接詞 I

不同於對等連接詞所連接的詞在詞性或文法作用上要有對等關係，從屬連接詞的功用在於引導副詞子句，其所連接的子句有主從關係。

表時間	1. when, while, as
	2. after, before, since
	3. as soon as, no sooner...than ⇨「一…，就…」
	4. until ⇨「直到…」
表讓步	1. although = though = even though = even if
	2. no matter + wh- 疑問詞 = 疑問詞 -ever ⇨「不論…」
	3. whether ⇨「不論…」
表條件	1. if = in case　　2. unless　　3. as long as ⇨「只要…」

Examples:

<< 表時間 >> 1. When you come to Taipei, I'll take you to the zoo.
（當你來臺北時，我會帶你去動物園。）

2. He has lived here since he married.
（他自從結婚後就一直住在這裡。）

3. As soon as the robbers saw the police, they fled away.
（這些搶匪一看到警察就溜之大吉。）

4. I had no sooner hung up than the phone started to ring again.
= No sooner had I hung up than the phone started to ring again.
（我一掛上電話，它又響了。）

5. My father didn't turn off the radio until the program ended.
（我父親直到節目結束才會關掉收音機。）

<< 表讓步 >> 1. Although she is my best friend, I won't forgive her.
= Even though she is my best friend, I won't forgive her.
= Even if she is my best friend, I won't forgive her.
（即使她是我最好的朋友，我也不會原諒她。）

2. No matter what you do, I won't trust you anymore.
= Whatever you do, I won't trust you anymore.
（不論你做什麼，我都不會再相信你了。）

3. <u>Whether</u> the teacher helps him or not, he will fail in the exam.

（不論老師幫不幫他，他這次考試都會不及格。）

<< 表條件 >> 1. If he doesn't come, you have to make a speech for him.

= <u>In case</u> he doesn't come, you have to make a speech for him.

（要是他不來，你要代替他演講。）

2. Lilly won't come to the practice <u>unless</u> her broken leg recovers.

（除非 Lilly 斷腿痊癒，否則她不會來參加練習。）

3. <u>As long as</u> we have hope, there is nothing we cannot achieve.

（只要心存希望，沒有什麼事是不能達成的。）

填入適當的從屬連接詞。

1. _____ you like jogging or not, you have to join the road running race next Sunday.

2. No matter _____ David goes, he always brings his dog with him.

3. I've been playing the online game "Lineage" _____ I was eighteen years old.

4. _____ the man left our convenience store, we found that he had stolen some chewing gum.

5. All the students screamed _____ the earthquake struck.

6. You had better bring an umbrella _____ _____ it rains.

7. I won't go to the concert _____ you buy a ticket for me.

8. _____ _____ _____ she opened the windows, the cold air came in.

9. I will stand up for you whatever they criticize about your work.

= _____ _____ _____ they criticize about your work, I will stand up for you.

9-3 從屬連接詞 II

表結果	1. so (that) ⇨「所以…」
	2. so + Adj/Adv + that ⇨「如此…以致於…」
	3. such + a(n) + N + that ⇨「如此的…以致於…」
表目的	1. so that = in order that ⇨「以便…」
	2. for fear that ⇨「以防（萬一）…」
表原因	1. because, as 2. since = now that ⇨「既然…」
表狀態	1. as ⇨「像，依照」
	2. as if = as though ⇨「好像…」，後面引導的子句中動詞通常採假設語氣。

Examples:

<< 表結果 >> 1. The rain was so heavy that there were floods all over the streets.
（雨勢太大以致於街上到處淹水。）

2. *King Lear* is such a famous play that everyone knows it.
（李爾王是這樣一齣名劇，以致大家都知道它。）

<< 表目的 >> 1. Jim got up early so that he could catch the first train.
= Jim got up early in order that he could catch the first train.
（Jim 起得很早，以便可以趕上第一班火車。）

2. They took the umbrella with them for fear that it might rain.
（他們帶雨傘，以防萬一下雨。）

<< 表原因 >> 1. Because my parents are angry at my grades, I can't go out.
（因為我父母氣我考得不好，我不能出門。）

2. Since Susan didn't bring any money with her, I paid for her.
= Now that Susan didn't bring any money with her, I paid for her.
（既然 Susan 沒有帶錢，我就幫她付了。）

<< 表狀態 >> She talks as if she knew Japan very well.
= She talks as though she knew Japan very well.
（她說得好像她對日本十分了解似的。）

 Try This !

填入適當的從屬連接詞。

1. Mike always carries a gun ＿＿＿＿＿ ＿＿＿＿＿ ＿＿＿＿＿ someone will rob him.

2. This watch is ＿＿＿＿＿ expensive ＿＿＿＿＿ I can't afford it.

3. This is ＿＿＿＿＿ an expensive watch ＿＿＿＿＿ I can't afford it.

4. ＿＿＿＿＿ ＿＿＿＿＿ you are here, we can start the meeting right now.

5. My father won't go on a trip with us ＿＿＿＿＿ he hates to take a plane.

6. He borrowed lots of books from the library ＿＿＿＿＿ ＿＿＿＿＿ he could write a good report.

7. Look at Peter. He wears ＿＿＿＿＿ ＿＿＿＿＿ he were a soldier.

8. ＿＿＿＿＿ he doesn't love you anymore, why not leave him?

9. This game is ＿＿＿＿＿ easy ＿＿＿＿＿ everyone knows how to play.

9-4 準連接詞（轉折語）

準連接詞或稱轉折語，是具有連接子句或句子功能的副詞，並非是真的連接詞，因此在連接句子的時候，要加上對等連接詞 and 或者是分號（；）。請務必注意標點符號的使用。

而且，此外	besides, also, moreover, furthermore, in addition, what's more, likewise
然而，但是	however, nevertheless, still, though
因此；結果	therefore, hence, thus, as a result
否則，不然	otherwise
相反地；另一方面	on the contrary, by contrast, on the other hand
最重要的	most important of all
舉例	for example, for instance
換句話說	similarly, in other words, that is (to say)

Examples:

<< 而且 >>　　　1. The rent of this apartment is reasonable, and <u>moreover</u> the location is good.
　　　　　　　　　（這間公寓租金合理，而且地點亦佳。）

　　　　　　　　2. This restaurant provides good service; <u>in addition</u>, they serve free drinks.
　　　　　　　　　（這間餐廳服務很好，而且還提供免費飲料。）

<< 然而 >>　　　It's fun to swim in a river. <u>However</u>, it is also dangerous.
　　　　　　　　（在河裡游泳很有趣，然而也很危險。）

<< 因此；結果 >>　1. We won't be home in the evening; <u>therefore</u>, we will have our answering machine on.
　　　　　　　　　（我們傍晚不會在家，因此我們會打開答錄機。）

　　　　　　　　2. The coming typhoon is very powerful; <u>as a result</u>, we needn't go to work.
　　　　　　　　　（即將到來的颱風威力強大，因此我們不用上班。）

<< 否則 >>　　　Finish your work immediately. <u>Otherwise</u>, you'll be fired.
　　　　　　　　（立刻完成你的工作，否則你會被炒魷魚。）

<< 相反的 >>   He is thought to be in Taipei. <u>On the contrary</u>, he is at home.

（大家都以為他在臺北，相反地他是在家裡。）

<< 最重要的 >>   Exercise is a good way to keep you in shape. <u>Most important of all</u>, it is good for your health.

（運動是保持身材的良方。最重要的是，對健康有益。）

<< 舉例 >>   I like eating vegetables — carrots and green peppers, <u>for instance</u>.

（我很喜歡吃蔬菜，比方像紅蘿蔔與青椒。）

<< 換句話說 >>   Jim never burns the midnight oil. <u>In other words</u>, he never stays up late.

（Jim 從不挑燈夜戰；換句話說，他從不熬夜。）

Try This !

選出正確的答案。

1. Sam is sick and won't go to work today. _____, he won't be able to pick you up as usual.

    (A) Still   (B) As a result

    (C) However   (D) On the contrary

2. We should hand in our homework on time. _____, the teacher will get mad at us.

    (A) Otherwise   (B) Therefore   (C) Besides   (D) Similarly

I. 選出正確的答案。

☐ 1. She can understand whatever the teachers say, _____ she is a clever girl.

    (A) so   (B) but   (C) and   (D) for

☐ 2. My mother often asks us to eat carrot, _____ we like it or not.

    (A) what   (B) that   (C) whether   (D) where

☐ 3. _____ you or my brother rang the bell and then ran away.

    (A) Neither   (B) Either   (C) Both   (D) Nor

☐ 4. It is said that it is possible for her to win the singing contest; _____, she fails.

    (A) nevertheless   (B) therefore   (C) likewise   (D) meanwhile

☐ 5. Janet is _____ a strict teacher that no student dares to doze off in her class.

    (A) so   (B) such   (C) or   (D) while

☐ 6. It has been ten years _____ we last met.

    (A) since   (B) for   (C) if   (D) when

☐ 7. I hate exercising; _____, my sister is good at sports.

    (A) however   (B) unless   (C) whereas   (D) consequently

☐ 8. Joe is good at sports. _____, he can play basketball, baseball, and volleyball.

    (A) For instance   (B) In addition   (C) Meanwhile   (D) What's more

☐ 9. Jim _____ his brothers hates to play chess with their father.

    (A) or   (B) but   (C) as well as   (D) and

☐ 10. Although he is poor, _____ he is never ashamed of himself.

    (A) but   (B) ×   (C) however   (D) so

☐ 11. Edison still has to go to work today, _____ the typhoon is very strong.

    (A) if   (B) even   (C) when   (D) even if

☐ 12. You had better get up right now. _____, you will be late for work.

    (A) However   (B) Therefore   (C) Otherwise   (D) Whether

☐ 13. Not only I but also Jenny _____ to play online games in our free time.

    (A) like   (B) liked   (C) liking   (D) likes

II. 挑錯並改正。

( ) ＿＿＿＿＿＿＿ 14. ^(A)When ^(B)had Jack seen Rose ^(C)than he fell ^(D)in love with her.

( ) ＿＿＿＿＿＿＿ 15. ^(A)Despite ^(B)he was poor, he ^(C)never begged ^(D)for money.

( ) ＿＿＿＿＿＿＿ 16. Mother won't give you money ^(A)if you ^(B)tell her ^(C)what you want to do with ^(D)it.

( ) ＿＿＿＿＿＿＿ 17. We will go ^(A)not only to France ^(B)also to Italy ^(C)for our honeymoon. These two places are the ^(D)most attractive to us.

( ) ＿＿＿＿＿＿＿ 18. Amy is ^(A)known to be ^(B)kind to everyone; ^(C)still, she is a ^(D)kind-hearted person.

( ) ＿＿＿＿＿＿＿ 19. Neither George ^(A)or Mary ^(B)borrowed money ^(C)from me. It was Jim who ^(D)owed me the money.

III. 依照提示合併句子。

20. We all hate to work every day.
   We still have to work for money. *(although)*

   ⇨ ＿＿＿＿＿＿＿＿＿＿＿＿＿＿＿＿＿＿＿＿＿＿＿＿＿＿＿＿

21. She put on her finest dress to the party.
   She could attract people's attention. *(in order that)*

   ⇨ ＿＿＿＿＿＿＿＿＿＿＿＿＿＿＿＿＿＿＿＿＿＿＿＿＿＿＿＿

22. Jimmy and I will go with you.
   You pay the bus fare for us. *(as long as)*

   ⇨ ＿＿＿＿＿＿＿＿＿＿＿＿＿＿＿＿＿＿＿＿＿＿＿＿＿＿＿＿

23. He found a lost purse.
   He sent it to the police station. *(as soon as)*

   ⇨ ＿＿＿＿＿＿＿＿＿＿＿＿＿＿＿＿＿＿＿＿＿＿＿＿＿＿＿＿

10–1　倒裝句 (Inverted Sentence)

在英文裡，為了強調句子中的某一個部份，會將句子的結構稍作改變。通常改變的方式是將要強調的部份移至句首，然後再做主詞與動詞的倒裝（也就是主詞與動詞的位置對調）。這樣的句型，我們稱為「倒裝句」。

一、地方副詞的倒裝句

地方副詞倒裝句的肯定句型：

一般直述句　　S + V + Adv（地方副詞）

改為倒裝句　　Adv（地方副詞）+ V + S

Examples:

1. A supermarket stands <u>opposite our school</u>.
   ⇨ <u>Opposite our school</u> <u>stands</u> a supermarket.
   （我們學校對面是家超市。）

2. A beautiful girl sits <u>beside Jason</u>.
   ⇨ <u>Beside Jason</u> <u>sits</u> a beautiful girl.
   （一個漂亮女生坐在 Jason 旁邊。）

主詞若為代名詞，則主詞與動詞不須倒裝：

句型變成 Adv（地方副詞）+ S + V

Examples:

1. He is <u>there</u>.　　　　　（他在那裡。）
   ⇨ <u>There</u> he is. ⇨ he 為代名詞，故不須倒裝。

2. She fell <u>off the tree</u>.　　（她從樹上摔下來了。）
   ⇨ <u>Off the tree</u> she fell. ⇨ she 為代名詞，故不須倒裝。

二、only 的倒裝句

一般含有 only 的直述句句型：S + V + only + Adv 片語或子句

改為倒裝句⇨ Only + Adv 片語或子句 + (1) be + S

(2) 助動詞 + S + 原形 V

(3) have/has/had + S + PP

Examples:

1. Rose is happy <u>only when she is with Jack</u>.

   ⇨ <u>Only when Rose is with Jack</u> <u>is</u> <u>she</u> happy.

   （只有當與 Jack 在一起時，Rose 才開心。）

2. Janet can relax herself <u>only by traveling abroad</u>.

   ⇨ <u>Only by traveling abroad</u> <u>can</u> <u>Janet</u> relax herself.

   （只有藉著出國旅行，Janet 才能自我放鬆。）

3. He feels comfortable <u>only at his own home</u>.

   ⇨ <u>Only at his own home</u> <u>does</u> <u>he</u> feel comfortable. ⇨注意主詞前要加上 does！

   （只有在自己的家裡，他才會覺得舒適。）

4. I have seen the aliens <u>only once in my life</u>.

   ⇨ <u>Only once in my life</u> <u>have</u> <u>I</u> <u>seen</u> the aliens.

   （我這一生只看過一次外星人。）

請將下列句子改寫為倒裝句

1. The antique violin is in this case.

   ⇨ _____

2. He fell down.

   ⇨ _____

3. A rare and beautiful flower grows on the top of the mountain.

   ⇨ _____

4. You can become slim only by eating less and taking more exercise.

   ⇨ _____

5. Ella studies hard only when the exam is coming.

   ⇨ _____

6. Carol has been to the concert hall only once in her life.

   ⇨ _____

7. Bonny would join our trip only if you could persuade her.

   ⇨ _____

三、否定詞的倒裝句

> 否定詞的倒裝
> (1) 常見的否定詞：seldom（很少），rarely（鮮少），scarcely（幾乎不），
> little（幾乎沒有），hardly（幾乎不），
> never（絕不、從未），in no way（絕不；一點也不），
> by no means（絕不），under no circumstances（絕不），
> nowhere（任何地方都沒…）
> (2) 一般含有否定詞的直述句型：S + be + 否定詞/S + 否定詞 + V
> 　　改為倒裝句：(a) 否定詞 + be + S
> 　　　　　　　　(b) 否定詞 + 助動詞 + S + 原形 V
> 　　　　　　　　(c) 否定詞 + have/has/had + S + PP

Examples:

1. Betty is seldom late for school.
   ⇨ Seldom is Betty late for school.
   （Betty 絕少遲到。）

2. Lucy has rarely gotten first place in anything in her life.
   ⇨ Rarely has Lucy gotten first place in anything in her life.
   （Lucy 在她一生中幾乎沒得過第一名。）

3. I scarcely know this man.
   ⇨ Scarcely do I know this man. ⇨注意主詞前加上 do！
   （我幾乎不認識這個人。）

4. He will never fall in love with other girls.
   ⇨ Never will he fall in love with other girls.
   （他再也不會愛上其他的女孩了。）

5. They are by no means bad guys.
   ⇨ By no means are they bad guys.
   （他們絕對不是壞人。）

6. Mr. Lee could <u>hardly</u> resist the temptation of gambling.

   ⇨ <u>Hardly</u> <u>could</u> Mr. Lee resist the temptation of gambling.

   （李先生幾乎無法抗拒賭博的誘惑。）

7. These teenagers <u>little</u> knew about the complicated business dealings.

   ⇨ <u>Little</u> <u>did</u> these teenagers know about the complicated business dealings.

   （這些青少年對這個複雜的商業交易所知極少。）⇨注意倒裝句加上 did！

Try This !

I. 選出正確的答案。

☐ 1. Never _____ take back the time we've wasted.

   (A) we can   (B) can we   (C) we will   (D) will us

☐ 2. Jenny is a kind girl. _____ do harm to others.

   (A) She never   (B) Seldom do she   (C) Never does she   (D) She will

☐ 3. Little _____ Johnny _____ the problems between his parents.

   (A) does, understand   (B) that, understands

   (C) can, understands   (D) is, understand

☐ 4. Never _____ Grace seen such a handsome boy.

   (A) did   (B) has   (C) will   (D) is

II. 請將下面各句改寫為倒裝句。

1. Andy will by no means cheat in the exams.

   ⇨_____

2. Sandy told us little about what had happened.

   ⇨_____

3. Elisabeth is seldom able to make a decision by herself.

   ⇨_____

4. I have never seen such a beautiful place as Sun Moon Lake.

   ⇨_____

5. Leo rarely takes exercise.

   ⇨_____

10-2 附加問句 (Tag Question)

一、基本的附加問句用法

主要子句之後，所追加的問句，稱為「附加問句」，可譯為「不是嗎」、「對不對」或「對吧」。

> 附加問句的基本原則：
>
> (1) 主詞一律改代名詞，
>
> (2) 肯定改否定，否定改肯定，
>
> (3) 要注意時態與主要子句一致。

Examples:

1. That is a wonderful movie, isn't it?   （那是部好片，不是嗎？）
2. Ron can't roller-skate as well as Hank, can he?   （Ron 沒辦法溜冰溜得像 Hank 那樣好，對吧？）
3. Dr. Chen works in Taipei, doesn't he?   （陳醫生在臺北工作，不是嗎？）
4. Cathy has not finished the four tragedies by Shakespeare, has she?   （Cathy 還沒有讀完莎翁四大悲劇，對吧？）

> 主要子句中有否定意味的字時，附加問句要用肯定句。

Examples:

1. He seldom goes to the movies, does he?   （他很少去看電影，對吧？）
2. Debby has never been to Mt. Ali, has she?   （Debby 從來沒去過阿里山，對吧？）
3. Joe is by no means a liar, is he?   （Joe 絕對不是個騙子，不是嗎？）

> 如果出現 I/We + think/believe/feel/know + (that) + 子句時，附加問句以子句為準。
>
> 如果出現 I/We + *don't* + think/believe/feel/know + (that) + 子句時，附加問句一律用肯定。

Examples:

1. We think (that) the dog has saved the little boy, hasn't it?
   （我們認為這隻狗已經救了這個小男孩，對不對？）

2. I know (that) Jim fools around all day long, doesn't he?
   （我知道 Jim 整天都在鬼混，不是嗎？）

3. I don't believe (that) you are a police officer, are you?
   （我不相信你是位警察，不是嗎？）

4. We don't feel (that) the suspect is innocent, is he?
   （我們不覺得這個嫌疑犯是清白的，對嗎？）

Try This !

I. 選出正確的答案。

▢ 1. Emily stayed at home crying all day long yesterday, _____?

   (A) did she   (B) stay she   (C) didn't she   (D) not she

▢ 2. Nancy has few friends, _____?

   (A) does she   (B) doesn't she   (C) has she   (D) hasn't she

▢ 3. There is nothing wrong with it, _____?

   (A) isn't there   (B) is there   (C) isn't it   (D) is it

II. 請將以下各句加上附加問句。

1. I feel that the weather is going to change, _____?

2. Her dog eats a lot, _____?

3. We don't know Karen doesn't like chocolate cake, _____?

4. Alice will in no way trust you anymore, _____?

二、附加問句的特殊用法—祈使句

直述句為祈使句時，無論肯定或否定句，附加問句一律為 "will you"。

Ⓔxamples:
1. Stand up, <u>will you</u>? （站起來，好嗎？）
2. Please don't close the window, <u>will you</u>? （請別關窗子，好嗎？）

直述句是 Let me/Let us + 原形 V 時，附加問句也一律用 "will you"。

Ⓔxamples:
1. Let me do it myself, <u>will you</u>? （讓我自己來，好嗎？）
2. Let us do what we want, <u>will you</u>? （讓我們做我們想做的事，可以嗎？）

直述句是 Let's+ 原形 V 時，附加問句一律用 "shall we"。

Ⓔxamples:
1. Let's have some ice cream, <u>shall we</u>? （我們來吃些冰淇淋，好嗎？）
2. Let's practice this new song, <u>shall we</u>? （我們來練習這首新曲子，如何？）

直述句是 Let's not + 原形 V 時，附加問句一律用 "all right" 或 "OK"。

Ⓔxamples:
1. Let's not go to the park, <u>all right</u>? （我們不要去公園，好不好？）
2. Let's not watch TV, <u>OK</u>? （我們不要看電視，好不好？）

Try This !

請將以下各句加上附加問句。

1. Leave me alone, _____?
2. Let's watch our favorite talk show, _____?
3. Let us go out for a while, _____?
4. Let's not spend our holiday watching TV, _____?
5. Don't go to the beach when there is a typhoon coming, _____?

10-3 直接問句改為間接問句

以 wh- 疑問詞 (who/what/when/where/how) 為首的直接問句改間接問句：

(1) Wh- 疑問詞 + be + S ⇨ ... + wh- 疑問詞 + S + be

(2) Wh- 疑問詞 + 助動詞 + S + 原形 V ⇨ ... + wh- 疑問詞 + S + 情態助動詞 + 原形 V

(3) Wh- 疑問詞 + have/has/had + S + PP ⇨ ... + wh- 疑問詞 + S + have/has/had + PP

Examples:

1. What time is it?

   ⇨ Can you tell me what time it is?

   （你能告訴我現在幾點嗎？）

2. Where should Irene put her new computer?

   ⇨ Mom is thinking where Irene should put her new computer.

   （媽媽正在思考 Irene 該把電腦放到哪裡去。）

3. When do you usually play basketball?

   ⇨ Your dad wants to know when you usually play basketball.

   （你的父親想知道你通常何時去打籃球。）

4. How long has John been an author?

   ⇨ I would like to know how long John has been an author.

   （我想知道 John 當作家已經多久了。）

沒有疑問詞的直接問句，或答句為 "yes" 或 "no" 的問句，在改寫為間接問句時，要加 "if" 或 "whether" 來引導。

Examples:

1. Are you a pilot?

   ⇨ She wants to know if you are a pilot.

   （她想知道你是不是飛行員。）

2. Did Amy take a bus to the office yesterday?

   ⇨ The boss asked whether <u>Amy took</u> a bus to the office the day before.

   （老闆問 Amy 昨天是不是搭公車到辦公室。）

3. Can Paul go out tonight?

   ⇨ I ask Paul if <u>he can go</u> out tonight.

   （我問 Paul 今晚可不可以出來。）

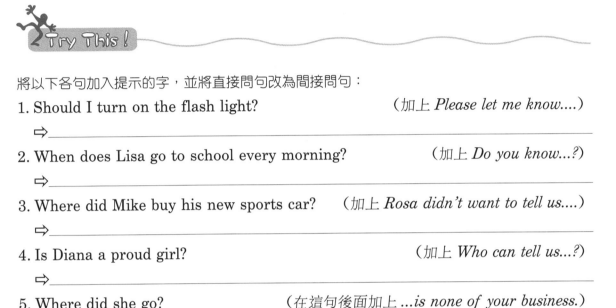

將以下各句加入提示的字，並將直接問句改為間接問句：

1. Should I turn on the flash light?　　　　　　　（加上 *Please let me know....*）

   ⇨ _____

2. When does Lisa go to school every morning?　　（加上 *Do you know...?*）

   ⇨ _____

3. Where did Mike buy his new sports car?　　（加上 *Rosa didn't want to tell us....*）

   ⇨ _____

4. Is Diana a proud girl?　　　　　　　　　　（加上 *Who can tell us...?*）

   ⇨ _____

5. Where did she go?　　　　　（在這句後面加上 *...is none of your business.*）

   ⇨ _____

I. 選出正確的答案。

☐ 1. Tom didn't want to whitewash the big fence, _____?
(A) was he   (B) does he   (C) will he   (D) did he

☐ 2. Many people want to know when and where _____.
(A) was the kid lost   (B) the kid was lost
(C) will the kid lose   (D) the kid be lost

☐ 3. I think that the thief should be severely punished, _____?
(A) shouldn't he   (B) don't I   (C) do I   (D) should he

☐ 4. What will he do? Can you tell me? （合併成一句）
(A) Can you tell me what will he do?   (B) Can you tell me what he will do?
(C) Will you tell me what can he do?   (D) Will you tell me what he can do?

☐ 5. Where did Mike go? I don't know that. （合併成一句）
(A) I don't know where did Mike go.   (B) I don't know where Mike goes.
(C) I don't know where Mike went.   (D) I don't know that Mike went.

☐ 6. True love exits only when two people have true hearts, _____?
(A) doesn't it   (B) does it   (C) don't they   (D) do they

☐ 7. Where is my cell phone? Do you remember that? （合併成一句）
(A) Do you remember where is my cell phone?
(B) Do you remember that is my cell phone?
(C) Do you remember where my cell phone is?
(D) Do you remember my cell phone is where?

II. 將下列句子改為倒裝句。

8. We will believe your words only when you stop telling lies.
⇨ _____

9. The beautiful roses are in full bloom in Mr. Gale's garden.
⇨ _____

10. The famous and popular movie star seldom appears in public places.
⇨ _____

11. Ella is never late for school.
⇨ _____

12. You can get better grades only by studying harder.

    ⇨ _____

13. Rachel will by no means betray her best friend.

    ⇨ _____

14. The school bus comes here.

    ⇨ _____

III. 從 A-K 中為下列句子挑選適當的附加問句。

15. "Swatch" is a popular brand among young people, _____?

16. Ancient Egyptians used perfume to purify their bodies as well as their mind, _____?

17. Turn off the lights and computers before you leave the office, _____?

18. Let's go to the beach and have some fun, _____?

19. Let's not go into the deep and dark forest, _____?

20. Hip hop has become the main stream of popular music, _____?

21. Lee often burns the midnight oil preparing for the graduation exam, _____?

22. Jason hardly goes to work by taxi, _____?

23. We're going to have heavy rain, _____?

24. There is going to be a violent argument between the boys and the girls, _____?

25. Allen can play both basketball and volleyball very well, _____?

A. hasn't it	B. shall we	C. didn't they	D. aren't we	E. can't he
F. doesn't he	G. all right	H. isn't it	I. does he	J. will you
K. isn't there				

IV. 將下列中文句子翻譯成英文。

26. Jean 問老師 , 地理是不是個困難的科目。

    _____

27. 你能告訴我 Roger 昨天晚上做了什麼嗎？

    _____

28. 沒有人知道籃球比賽何時會開始。

    _____

29. 你媽媽問我你在學校有沒有用功讀書。

    _____

30. 我們想知道是誰偷了這個珍貴的古董花瓶。

    _____

Answer Key

Chapter 1　句子的結構

page 3

Try This!

I. 1. B　2. A　3. A　4. A　5. B

II. 1. A　2. C　3. E　4. D　5. B

page 5

Try This!

I. 1. A　2. B

II. 1. fetches sports magazines　2. lent, some money

page 7

Try This!

1. makes　2. belongs　3. seems　4. serve(s)

[解析] 1. news 這個字為不可數名詞。

page 9

Try This!

I. 1. A　2. B　3. B　4. B　5. B

II. 1. are　2. makes　3. want, is　4. is　5. are

page 11

Try This!

1. borrows　2. troubles　3. refuses

pages12-13

Test & Review

I. 1. A　2. C　3. A　4. D　5. B　6. D　7. C　8. B　9. D　10. A

II. 11. C　12. D　13. B　14. D　15. D

III. 16. as, as, doesn't, when　17. girl, likes, sending, to　18. and, is　19. Half, were/are　20. is,
　　　 wants

[解析] I. 9. well 不是形容詞，是副詞。句型：taste + 物 + Adj。

　　　II. 12. 是 money（受詞）被偷，不是 I（主詞）被偷，stolen 修飾受詞，是為 OC（受詞補語）。

　　　III. 19. 這裡的 committee 是集合名詞，依中文語意「委員們」推知用複數較適合。

　　　　20. to love and to be loved「愛人和被愛」為同一件事，視為單數主詞。

Chapter 2　時態

page 15

Try This!

1. reads　2. doesn't, like　3. Do; take　4. helps, help　5. is　6. rises

page 16

Try This!

1. is, playing　2. are, discussing　3. am, talking

page 17

Try This!

1. C　2. B　3. A

page 19

Try This!

I. 1. D　2. A　3. B　4. B　5. A

II. 1. have, playing　2. hasn't, yet　3. have, seen　4. has, gone, to

page 21

Try This!

1. Did, take 2. used, to, get 3. ate/had, now 4. Did, rain 5. didn't, make 6. went

page 22

Try This!

1. When, got, ringing 2. was, singing, was, dancing

page 23

Try This!

1. C 2. D

page 24

Try This!

I. 1. D 2. D

II. 1. were, having 2. had, been, traveling 3. had, been

page 25

Try This!

1. Will, become 2. coming 3. going, do

page 26

Try This!

I. 1. A 2. B 3. D

II. 1. There, will, be 2. will, be, jogging

page 27

Try This!

1. comes, will, have, built 2. will, have, been, working, comes

pages 28-29

Test & Review

I. 1. D 2. A 3. B 4. C 5. A 6. C 7. B 8. D 9. B 10. D

II. 11. went, had, been, preparing 12. study, will, enter 13. has, gone, to

III. 14. E 15. C 16. F 17. B 18. D 19. G 20. A

Chapter 3　語態

page 31

Try This!

1. was, finished 2. were, stolen

page 33

Try This!

I. 1. C 2. A 3. D 4. A 5. A

II. 1. was, stolen 2. will, be 3. isn't, invited

page 34

Try This!

1. are, being, questioned 2. were, being, washed 3. am, being, blamed

page 35

Try This!

1. has, been, seen 2. will, have, been, fixed/repaired 3. had been sold

page 36

Try This!

1. Will your dirty clothes be washed by you tomorrow?

2. A strange man with a gun was seen to go into the president's residence by me.

page 37

Try This!

1. Was the car washed by Peggy last week?

2. Was this vase broken by you?

page 38

Try This!

1. Where should the toys be put by little Johnny?

2. By whom were you taught English?

page 39

Try This!

1. Let the doorbell be rung.

2. Joe was not seen to play baseball by Alice this afternoon.

pages 40~41

Test & Review

I. 1. D 2. A 3. B 4. A 5. C 6. A 7. C 8. D

II. 9. By, whom, shot 10. not, be, caught 11. be, held 12. was, seen, to, play 13. How, be 14. Is, used

15. has, been, repaired/fixed

III. 16. Don't let the light be turned off when I am reading.

17. A note was left on my desk.

18. Has the medicine been taken by Jim?

19. Jordan was called "Air Jordan" by his fans.

20. Let the homework be finished at once.

21. The waste paper is being recycled by my students.

22. The rare opportunity will not be given up by them.

23. Why was the toy robot thrown away by David?

24. Mary's sister was heard to cry in her room by Mary.

25. By whom were cars invented?

[解析] I. 3. 這一題的中文翻譯是「木已成舟」，也就是「已經完成的事不能再重來」的意思。所以要選 be undone。

III. 21. 廢紙是不可數名詞，所以 be 動詞用 is。

Chapter 4　助動詞

page 43

Try This!

I. 1. So have I. 2. Neither did George. 3. Neither is Tim.

II. 1. didn't, did 2. did

page 45

Try This!

I. 1. Will 2. should 3. shouldn't 4. will 5. should 6. Will 7. will

II. 1. shouldn't, have, thrown 2. Will, move

page 47

Try This!

I. 1. could 2. can't/couldn't 3. Can/Could 4. can't/couldn't 5. couldn't

II. 1. cannot, but, wear 2. can't, have, gone

page 49

Try This!

I. 1. would 2. may 3. may

II. 1. would, rather, than 2. may, well 3. may/might, as, well, as

page 51

Try This!

I. 1. must/have to go 2. have to make 3. mustn't go 4. must have eaten

5. mustn't tell 6. must have lost

II. 1. must, have 2. have, to 3. Must, needn't 4. have to

pages 52-53　　**Test & Review**

I. 1. B 2. A 3. C 4. D 5. A 6. A 7. C 8. D 9. A 10. B 11. D 12. D 13. C 14. A 15. D

II. 16. E 17. A 18. C 19. D 20. B

III. 21. B, buy 22. D, rush 23. A, may/might as well 24. A, shouldn't 25. C, had to 26. A, Would

[解析] I. 2. 評斷一個人不能光憑外表，所以「可能」錯怪別人。might 在「可能」的意義上比 must 來得適切。
11. 「我很確定他忘記了」，所以「打電話給我」這件事情是他應該做的，卻沒有做，要用 should have PP 的句型。

Chapter 5　假設語氣

page 55　　**Try This!**

I. 1. C 2. D 3. A 4. B

II. 1. were, would/could/might help 2. read, would/could/might learn about

III. 1. would, if, saw 2. were, could, go

page 57　　**Try This!**

I. 1. B 2. C 3. A 4. A

II. 1. had found, could have given 2. had rained, would have

III. 1. had, been, have, let 2. would, be, had, rained 3. had, might

page 59　　**Try This!**

I. 1. C 2. B 3. C

II. 1. Had, have 2. were, to 3. should, may/might/would/will

page 61　　**Try This!**

I. 1. A 2. D 3. B 4. A

II. 1. lived 2. were

[解析] I. 4. 這題最困難的地方在於分辨 nothing 與 anything 的使用方式，千萬記得，anything 只能使用在否定與疑問句裡。另外，「看起來像」的動詞 look 為現在式，表示他「現在」看起來對這件事一無所知，所以 as if 後面的條件句要使用過去式。

pages 62-63　　**Test & Review**

I. 1. C 2. C 3. C 4. A 5. A 6. C 7. C 8. B

II. 9. didn't, have, might, be 10. had, listened, fought 11. hadn't, have, been

12. should, would/will, Should, would/will 13. were, would, be 14. had, seen, would, know

III. 15. B 16. A 17. D 18. E 19. C

Chapter 6　關係子句

page 65　　**Try This!**

I. 1. who 2. whom 3. who

II. 1. That boy who is sitting under the tree likes to play golf.

2. The beautiful girl whose eyes are blue is Pinky.

page 67

Try This!

I. 1. The river which flows through our town is polluted.

2. Have you seen a cat whose eyes are green?

3. Gina wants to take care of the poor kitten whose leg is hurt.

4. Helen wore the blue sweater which her mom bought for her last week.

II. 1. which, bought 2. which, are 3. steal, whose

page 68

Try This!

I. 1. The woman and her cat that are sitting on the bench look very peaceful.

2. The woman and her car that the truck hit are still fine.

3. The man and the statue that are standing side by side look like twin brothers.

4. The beauty and the snake that we saw at the market last week are giving a performance together in the square.

page 70

Try This!

I. 1. My mom, who is a tender woman, takes good care of us.

2. Mr. Lin, who teaches us Chinese, is a very serious teacher.

3. The *Mona Lisa*, which was created by Leonardo da Vinci, is a beautiful masterpiece.

II. 1. which 2. whom 3. which 4. which 5. whom ·6. which

[解析] I. 3. 這不是腦筋急轉彎，Mona Lisa 是「一幅」人物「畫」，所以關代還是用 which。

page 71

Try This!

I. 1. X, that 2. ○ 3. X, whom 4. X, whose 5. ○ 6. X, whose 7. ○

II. 1. Who is the boy that plays computer games over there?

2. Helen is the very person that I want to choose as the class leader.

[解析] I. 4. 記得 whose 是不能用 that 來代替的。

6. 「他的音樂」，關代只有 whose 可以用。就算關代不是 whose，在非限定句型中，that 也不能當關代使用。

page 75

Try This!

1. where 2. where 3. when 4. where 5. when

page 77

Try This!

1. The cake we bought yesterday is very delicious.

2. This is the man giving us the book.

3. The cat always chasing a mouse is now taking a sun bath.

4. The lady reading the novel in the café is my aunt.

pages 78-79

Test & Review

I. 1. B 2. B 3. D 4. A 5. B 6. C 7. A 8. C 9. B 10. C

II. 11. shoes, are 12. The, girl, whom/that 13. whose, are, is 14. Those/People, who, are

15. who/that, has, been

III. 16. B 17. D 18. A 19. C

IV. 20. Mr. Lee was the first one that left the office yesterday.

21. Flora is the only friend that I trust.

22. Those/People who live in big cities are usually unfriendly.

Chapter 7   不定詞與助動詞

page 81

Try This!

I. 1. turning 2. playing 3. to sing 4. marrying 5. to win

II. 1. hopes, to, be 2. stealing, selling 3. to, hurt

page 83

Try This!

1. bringing 2. to hand 3. fighting 4. criticizing 5. to return 6. locking 7. to run 8. to say

page 85

Try This!

1. Betty is experienced enough to handle this difficult task.

2. They were too frightened to describe what they saw.

3. The little boy kept making loud noise so as to watch cartoons.

4. In order to stop George from selling his house, Elvira ran after him.

page 88

Try This!

I. 1. talking 2. hearing 3. defeating 4. jogging 5. crying 6. living 7. building

8. singing 9. looking 10. eating

II. 1. worth, encouraging 2. trouble, jogging 3. come, near, to, giving 4. complaining

page 89

Try This!

1. Is it relaxing to take a long walk?

2. It may take more time to take a bus to work.

3. It can enrich our mind to read more classics.

4. Does it take long time to make good friends?

page 91

Try This!

1. embarrassed 2. enjoying 3. punished 4. eaten 5. robbing 6. boring

7. broken 8. frightening 9. saying, staring 10. untouched.

page 93

Try This!

1. Being too tired, she rested her head on my shoulder to take a rest.

2. Maria sat on the sofa, reading stories to her children.

3. (After) finishing their final exam, all the students cried out loudly and jumped around happily.

4. Lisa slept in her room, snoring loudly.

page 96

Try This!

1. The woman (being) blamed for her being unfriendly has two children.

2. The train (having been) crowded with people is destined for Taichung.

3. The plane (being) filled with rice and vegetable is going to take off.

4. The factory having opened for more than 20 years produces chips.

5. Catching a cold, Joseph couldn't join the party last night.

6. When compared with his brother, he is considered to be more cunning.

= (Being) Compared with his brother, he is considered to be more cunning.

pages 97-99   **Test & Review**

I. 1. B 2. A 3. B 4. A 5. D 6. C 7. C 8. B 9. A 10. D 11. C 12. C

II. 13. To, sleep, is, impossible 14. having, talked 15. visiting 16. weep 17. so, as, to 或 in, order, to 18. nice

III. 19. B, regretting 20. A, To make 21. B, set up 22. A, so

IV. 23. comes, to, jogging 24. Not, knowing, to, ask 25. having, finished, can, eat 26. too, to 27. To, say, to, do 28. worth/worthwhile, buying

[解析] I. 8. prefer A to B 中，A、B 均為名詞，碰到動詞都要改成名詞，不要被 to 騙了。

10. A 選項不是被動語態的分詞構句（很單純的關係子句）；B 選項找不到動詞；C 選項不是被動語態的形（PP）。D 是標準的被動語態分詞片語 killed by sb。

III. 22. honest 並不是名詞，而是形容詞，記得句型 such + a(n) + N + that 或 so + Adj + that。

Chapter 8　形容詞、副詞與比較級

page 101   **Try This!**

1. a large Italian wooden bookcase

2. an expensive clothes hanger

3. a beautiful tall young lady

4. a small fat gray bird

5. a huge sweet orange

page 103   **Try This!**

1. terribly 2. hard 3. Unfortunately 4. sometimes 5. how 6. busily 7. tomorrow 8. hardly 9. inside 10. How

page 105   **Try This!**

I. 1. My grandfather goes to bed as early as my grandmother.

2. Mike doesn't have so many cars as Jim.

3. He tried to finish the work as quickly as possible.

4. Joe owns as many houses as Dick.

5. I work as fast as I can./I've worked as fast as I can.

II. 1. could, play, as, well, as 2. as, great, as

[解析] II. 1. 這裡的比較是副詞比較，「打得好」的「好」形容詞是 good，副詞是 well，不要搞混了。

page 107   **Try This!**

I. 1. My cousin is less handsome than I.

2. A: Ray is junior to me.

B: Ray is younger than I./I am older than Ray.

3. I get up earlier in the morning than Tina.

II. 1. much, higher 2. more, and, more, beautiful 3. superior, better, than

page 109 **Try This!**

I. 1. It is the most boring movie that I have ever seen.

2. Camping in the mountains was one of the worst experiences in my life.

3. *Time* is the most attracting magazine in this bookstore.

II. 1. the, most, confident 2. the, strongest 3. the, least

page 112 **Try This!**

1. A: She is more diligent than any other student in our class.

B: No other student in our class is more diligent than she.

2. To Jack, nothing is as important as making money.

3. My sister's CDs are twice the number of mine.

4. Lisa is the younger of the two women./Tina is the older of the two women.

5. The less you smoke, the more healthy you will be.

6. Maria sings more beautifully than all the other students in my class.

7. Nobody among us drives more safely than Tim.

[解析] 3. 所比較的是「數量」，可數名詞用 number，不可數名詞用 amount，本題 CD 可數。

pages 113-115 **Test & Review**

I. 1. B 2. D 3. A 4. B 5. A 6. C 7. C 8. A 9. B 10. D 11. C 12. B

II. 13. ten, times, as 14. the, hottest

15. more, attractive, any, other, as, attractive

III. 16. C, difficult 17. B, high 18. D, younger 19. A, much the 20. D, city/C, all the

IV. 21. worse, than 22. faster, easier 23. one, of, the, most, popular 24. as, strong, as 25. The, more, the, more 26. Nobody, as/so, as, more, humorous, than, all, the, other

[解析] I. 9. 比較級與最高級前面修飾的副詞要看意思使用，不是隨便亂加。這裡最合句義的是 by far（到目前為止）。

III. 16. find + it + Adj，但是 difficulty 是名詞，必須改成 difficult。

18. 這裡 twice 修飾後面的比較級，表示「兩倍的年輕」，因為後面有 than，young 要改成 younger。

Chapter 9 連接詞

page 117 **Try This!**

I. 1. for 2. so 3. and 4. or 5. but 6. so 7. or 8. but

II. 1. Either you or John is to blame for the fault./Either John or you are to blame for the fault.

2. Elsa is good at singing as well as composing.

3. Neither Martha nor Alice knew what to do.

[解析] II. 3. Neither A nor B 最大的陷阱就在於這個片語本身已經有否定意味，因此在合併時，不可以把 didn't 寫出來，know 也要寫成過去式。

page 119 **Try This!**

1. whether 2. where 3. since 4. After/As 5. when

6. in, case 7. unless 8. as, soon, as 9. No, matter, what

page 121   **Try This!**

1. for, fear, that 2. so, that 3. such, that 4. Now, that

5. because 6. so, that 7. as, if/though 8. Since 9. so, that

page 123   **Try This!**

1. B 2. A

pages 124-125   **Test & Review**

I. 1. D 2. C 3. B 4. A 5. B 6. A 7. A 8. A 9. C 10. B 11. D 12. C 13. D

II. 14. A, No sooner

15. A, Although/Though/Even if/Even though

16. A, unless

17. B, but (also)

18. C, that's to say/in other words

19. A, nor

III. 20. Although we all hate to work every day, we still have to work for money.

21. She put on her finest dress to the party in order that she could attract people's attention.

22. Jimmy and I will go with you as long as you pay the bus fare for us.

23. As soon as he found a lost purse, he sent it to the police station.

[解析] I. 7. 在空格前後分別出現分號（；）與逗點，表示這裡要的是轉折語，如果是 whereas，整句就必須寫成 I hate exercising whereas my sister is good at sports.

II. 16. 這一句不是文法問題，而是語意問題。用 if 是「是否」，句意不通，unless 意義才會通順。

18. kind to everyone 與 kind-hearted 意義一樣，因此把 C 換成 that's to say 或 in other words。

Chapter 10   倒裝句、附加問句、直接問句與間接問句

page 128   **Try This!**

1. In this case is the antique violin.

2. Down he fell.

3. On the top of the mountain grows a rare and beautiful flower.

4. Only by eating less and taking more exercise can you become slim.

5. Only when the exam is coming does Ella study hard.

6. Only once in her life has Carol been to the concert hall.

7. Only if you could persuade Bonny would she join our trip.

page 130   **Try This!**

I. 1. B 2. C 3. A 4. B

II. 1. By no means will Andy cheat in the exams.

2. Little did Sandy tell us about what had happened.

3. Seldom is Elisabeth able to make a decision by herself.

4. Never have I seen such a beautiful place as Sun Moon Lake.

5. Rarely does Leo take exercise.

page 132

Try This!

I. 1. C 2. A 3. B

II. 1. isn't it 2. doesn't it 3. does she 4. will she

page 133

Try This!

1. will you 2. shall we 3. will you 4. OK/all right 5. will you

page 135

Try This!

1. Please let me know if/whether I should turn on the flash light.

2. Do you know when Lisa goes to school every morning?

3. Rosa didn't want to tell us where Mike bought his new sports car.

4. Who can tell us if/whether Diana is a proud girl?

5. Where she went is none of your business.

pages 136-137

Test & Review

I. 1. D 2. B 3. A 4. B 5. C 6. A 7. C

II. 8. Only when you stop telling lies will we believe your words.

9. In Mr. Gale's garden are the beautiful roses in full bloom.

10. Seldom does the famous and popular movie star appear in public places.

11. Never is Ella late for school.

12. Only by studying harder can you get better grades.

13. By no means will Rachel betray her best friend.

14. Here comes the school bus.

III. 15. H 16. C 17. J 18. B 19. G 20. A 21. F 22. I 23. D 24. K 25. E

IV. 26. Jean asked the teacher if/whether geography was a difficult subject.

27. Can you tell me what Roger did last night?

28. Nobody knows when the basketball game will begin.

29. Your mother asked me if/whether you studied hard at school.

30. We would like to/want to know who stole this valuable antique vase.

Linguaskill 領思高頻字彙

睿言商英編輯團隊　編著
Chris Jordan　審閱

備考領思，選擇《Linguaskill 領思高頻字彙》的 **4** 大理由：

1. 最輕鬆：

集結領思高頻字彙 (CEFR A1 到 B1)，讓你一本就能快速掌握考試範圍！

2. 最雙效：

符合國內入學測驗單字範圍，讓你準備領思同時也能備考升學考試！領思成績還可登錄學習歷程檔案！

3. 最道地：

提供美、英式單字發音音檔，熟悉不同口音，讓你放眼世界，打造 Global Englishes！

4. 最實用：

例句情境取材貼近生活，打造素養精神，讓你學以致用！

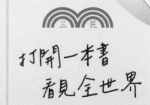